A CRIME REMEMBERED

Jeffrey Ashford

ATLANTIC LARGE PRINT

Chivers Press, Bath, England.
John Curley & Associates Inc.,
South Yarmouth, Mass., USA.

Library of Congress Cataloging in Publication Data

Ashford, Jeffrey, 1926–
  A crime remembered / Jeffrey Ashford.
    p.   cm.—(Atlantic large print)
  ISBN 1–55504–856–0 (lg. print)
  1. Large type books.   I. Title.
[PR6060.E43C75 1989]   88–35029
823'.914—dc19   CIP

British Library Cataloguing in Publication Data

Ashford, Jeffrey, 1926–
  A crime remembered
  I. Title
  823'.914 [F]

  ISBN 0–7451–9471–0

This Large Print edition is published by Chivers Press, England, and John Curley & Associates, Inc, U.S.A. 1989

Published in the British Commonwealth by arrangement with William Collins Sons & Co Ltd and in the U.S.A. with St. Martin's Press Inc

U.K. Hardback ISBN 0 7451 9471 0
U.S.A. Softback ISBN 1 55504 856 0

A CRIME REMEMBERED

For generations the Tourkvilles had owned Highland Place and it was love for his inheritance which had made the present owner, Edward Pierre Darcy Tourkville, dedicate his life to rebuilding the estate which his father had almost lost through bad management. Success seemed within his grasp when he was brought face to face with the past; a brutal, murderous, wartime past, which threatened to destroy all his work and put not only the survival of the estate once more at risk, but his own survival as well. Relentlessly the past caught up with him in the person of Detective-Sergeant Noyes. But did Noyes represent Nemesis or salvation? Were there ever circumstances in which murder could be justified, however intolerable the stress a man faced?

A CRIME REMEMBERED

CHAPTER ONE

The middle-aged, yawning DC interrupted the interminable descriptions of the PC's conquests. 'Welland Road's the next on the left.'

'Yeah, I know.' The driver checked the rear-view mirror for following traffic, braked, changed down.

They passed an unloading van, badly parked, and turned into the gently curving Welland Road. 'Seems like they're always building,' said the DC, as he stared at a block of flats which was being erected in what had been the grounds of a large Edwardian house.

'Know what I was told they're going to cost?' The driver took his right hand off the wheel and jerked his thumb at the building site. 'Eighty grand and going up to a hundred for the top flat with a view. A view of what is what I'd like to know.'

'The roofs of north Etrington.'

'Talking about views, there was this little blonde, wouldn't walk near a haystack to look at her, who I met . . .'

The DC saw the small group of onlookers first. 'That must be Hesketh Mansions over to the left.'

They double parked by a red Jaguar. 'Hang on here, will you?' said the DC. 'I shouldn't

1

be all that long.'

'No can do,' replied the PC quickly. 'In less than an hour and a half I've a date with a number who makes the blood boil just to look at her.'

'Then watch you don't steam right away.'

The PC impatiently waited for the DC to climb out and shut the door, then he drove off at speed. The DC walked past the onlookers—who did not appear to be discouraged by the fact that they had nothing and no one other than a uniform PC to stare at—nodded hullo to the PC and asked where the action was. The PC directed him round to the utility area, which lay behind and to one side of the square between the two arms of the large block of flats.

The body had landed by the side of a wooden hut in which was stored the gardening equipment; that it had not been discovered earlier was due to the fact that the hut concealed it from any casual glance.

He stared at the body without any particular emotion, inured to the evidence of mortality by years of having to deal with unnatural death. The PC who'd been standing guard pointed up and to his right. 'He fell down from there.'

The DC looked up. On each of the six floors there were small balconies, in pairs, spaced out at regular intervals; many of the balconies had potted plants growing on them,

2

but not the one the PC had indicated. 'Has he been identified yet?'

'John Harris. He's been living here for something like ten months.'

'What about a family?'

'There's none been with him. My oppo's had a quick word with some of the other residents and it seems like no one knows much about him. Didn't want to, moreover.'

'Why not?'

The PC removed his helmet and brushed the back of a hand across his forehead, as if wiping away sweat, but the day was overcast and the wind, considering this was the middle of May, sharp. 'People didn't take to him; one thing that got up their noses, he entertained a succession of young men.'

'Like that, was it?'

'So some old biddy said; gave the place a bad tone.'

'Hasn't she heard we're all liberated these days?' The DC looked back at the body. Although the back of the head had suffered severe damage, the face had not. It was a pinched, weak face which held a rat-like quality; a man who had worked from corners. His clothes had an expensive look to them, but the multi-coloured hand-knitted cardigan, in a striking geometrical pattern, was gaping sufficiently to show food stains on the roll-neck shirt; his chin was heavily stubbled, suggesting that he hadn't shaved for

3

quite a time prior to his death. Most people who lived in north Etrington did not realize that it was possible to live without shaving at least once a day. 'Has the doc been out?'

'Not yet, although he was called first thing.'

'He'll tell you he's a very busy man . . . Have we anything to suggest a time of death?'

'Not that I know of.' The PC grinned. 'But surely that's why the clever brigade's been called out?'

'Sure, only they were all out, using their brains, so I got sent instead. I see the french windows are open on to the balcony. Wouldn't be surprising if he'd had a skinful and walked out and over the rails without ever realizing what was happening.'

'What a smooth way to go! Don't know anything about it.'

'How d'you know that? I read a theory that after death everything's reversed so normal life's agony and it's only painful times that are pleasant.'

'Stick to religion and angels.'

'Any idea who has the keys of the flat?'

'My oppo got a spare set from the caretaker, or whatever the odd-job man calls himself.'

'Where's your oppo?'

'Out front, staring at all the morons who are staring at him.'

The DC retraced his steps round the

building to the PC who was keeping the small crowd at a distance. He asked for, and was given, the key of Flat 3g.

The interior of the flat reminded him of the glossy magazines which depicted the homes of the trendy wealthy; there was a jumble of colours and styles designed to startle, especially those with some natural taste.

The sitting-room was large and furnished in leather and velvet. Rather like an up-market brothel, thought the DC. On one of the occasional tables there was a three-parts-empty bottle of Dimple Haig and a glass. A pretty clear indication that Harris had at least been drinking. The DC went through to the kitchen and found a clean glass, poured himself out a large whisky. He seldom had the chance to drink Dimple Haig.

He searched the flat and was surprised how few personal possessions there were.

★   ★   ★

Thomas stood just over six feet two inches tall, but a pronounced stoop almost drew his head down to the same level as the DC's. Long hairs curled out of his nose. He had announced that his christian name was John without the suggestion of a snigger, leaving the DC to suppose that he was as much of a fool as his parents had been.

'Knew him by sight, of course,' he said, in

his high-pitched, clipped voice. He wore a hacking jacket and corduroy trousers and from time to time he slapped an invisible riding switch against the side of his leg.

'But you don't know much about him?'

'Putting it bluntly, old man, I don't know a damn thing, by choice.'

'Why's that?'

'Never have any truck with his kind. They can say it's natural as often as they like, but in my book it remains bloody unnatural.'

'You're talking about the young men?'

'Well, I'm not talking about his grandmother.'

'I understand you heard something from his flat last night?'

'That's right. The good lady and I came back late . . .'

'What would you call late?'

'After midnight.'

'And?'

'I'm trying to tell you, ain't I?' Whack, went the imaginary switch. 'Had to pass his place, of course. There was a filthy row; trying to sing, from the sound of it. I was all for telling him to shut up, that we don't behave like that here, but the good lady wouldn't let me. Doesn't like trouble.'

'Could you judge what sort of a state he was in?'

'As drunk as a Maltese cook.'

*   *   *

Having questioned anyone who might reasonably have been thought able to help, and having learned very little, the DC returned to Flat 3g where he picked up the large brown envelopes in which he'd put all the papers he had found. He hoped, without much optimism, that a much more careful examination of the papers would provide an identification of the dead man's next-of-kin; unclaimed bodies created hell with the records.

He left the flat and went down and out to the street; he saw the doctor walk round the far end of the building. He hurried over to the red BMW and reached it as the doctor put his hand on the door-handle. 'DC Phibbs, sir.'

'Whatever it is, it'll have to wait.'

'Won't keep you a second. Can you give me an estimate of the time of death?'

'Between six and ten hours ago. And that's no more accurate than usual.'

'How does the death look?'

'How does death ever look? But if you mean the circumstances, everything's consistent with his having fallen from the balcony. Nothing more will be known until the PM.'

'Could he have been tight at the time?'

'There was certainly the scent of stale

7

alcohol about him . . . But that seems to be quite common.'

The DC, remembering the Dimple Haig, leaned back. 'Thanks, sir.'

The doctor climbed into the car and drove off.

CHAPTER TWO

Detective-Constable Noyes resentfully wound the form into the typewriter. Napoleon's armies had marched on their stomachs, the modern police shuffled along on their paperwork. He began to type.

The door of the general room opened and the round face of the detective-sergeant looked in. 'Are you the only erk around?'

'That's right, skipper. Always the first to arrive and the last to leave.'

Burrow made a derisive noise before he opened the door more fully and entered. He threaded his way between the overcrowded desks and tables, cabinets, untidy piles of files and books, and the odd item of recovered property which should have been under lock and key in the property room, to sit on the corner of Noyes's desk. 'I've a job for you.'

'Just what I needed, since I've only a couple of dozen cases on my plate at the moment.'

'Not complaining, are you?' Burrow grinned. He had a comfortable, pleasant face that correctly suggested his normal easy-going manner. 'Etrington's sent down a request for a witness statement.'

'Where's Etrington?'

'Somewhere west of Birmingham; it's famous for its Morris dancers.'

'My favourite form of entertainment.'

'They've had a fatal and there's trouble learning anything about the dead man, in particular who's the next-of-kin. They've been through all his papers and the only reference which might offer a lead is a bit cryptic . . . But look at the request for yourself.'

Noyes took the Telex message and read through it. 'You call it cryptic? I'd call it a non-starter. E. P. D. T. Glinton. Sounds like the beginning of a dirty limerick.'

'It could be that someone who lives in either East or West Glinton has the initials E. P. D. T. So check through all the usual sources and if you come up with a name, ask him what he knows about John Harris, recently deceased.'

'Sarge, like I said, I'm busy . . .'

'And you can start moving now.'

'But I promised the wife I'd be back early tonight.'

'Will you never learn? Shows you've not been married long to make such a rash

9

promise . . . As quick as you like. Other force's problems don't do anything for our clear-up rate.' He slid off the desk and walked back to the door, his ill-fitting jacket riding up his neck as he moved.

'Shit!' said Noyes. Carol was not going to like this; not one little bit. He'd promised to take her out to one of the local Chinese restaurants for supper and if he stood her up she'd raise the roof . . .

Five years could do a lot to a marriage. Five years could dim even the brightest of the stars in the eyes. He wasn't the first man to discover that the most unlikely part of any fairy story was the bit about living happily ever after, but he did wonder how and why they'd reached their present, often strained relationship? After all, he made reasonable money and she worked in a dress shop and earned good commission. They had their own house—he was too smart to settle for a police house and then discover himself homeless on retirement—they ran a two-year-old Strada, she could dress like a princess because of the shop, they had video and hi-fi in the sitting-room, drink in the cupboard, and if they felt like eating out, they did so. Yet their rows had steadily become more frequent and bitter and he had begun to think of their marriage as becoming bracketed in the one-third destined to end in divorce rather than the two-thirds which should survive.

10

And although, when they were having one of their rows, it might still hurt to look at her and find her as beautiful and desirable as the day he'd married her, he wasn't going to accept responsibility for all that had gone wrong. He might be many things, but he wasn't weak.

He despised weakness. Life was about fighting. Fighting the form bully because he couldn't name his father and although one-parent families were said to be fashionable, the form bully had decreed otherwise; fighting the viral infection which had baffled the doctors and specialists and which had, for a mind-numbing time, threatened to leave him paralysed; fighting his way out of a background which seldom let anyone go because most were stupid enough to believe that easy money need not carry a cost . . .

He'd had to fight for Carol. Attractive and vivacious, she'd always attracted the men. He remembered Rodney with particular scorn. Rodney had pursued her with expensive gifts and lifestyle, paid for by his father's money. Yet he'd always spoken contemptuously about his father because the old boy never tried to make out that he was anyone other than a tough old bastard who still ate with his elbows on the table, even when living in a manor house . . .

He had to fight all the time at work, fight to

prove he was the best man, because there were more detective-constables than detective-sergeants and even fewer detective-inspectors. And this meant working all hours, even if that antagonized one's wife so much that she summoned up Judy of the glowing red hair, generous breasts, and eager body . . .

He stood up, angry to have wasted so much time in useless thoughts. He picked up the Telex message, left and went along the corridor to the 'library' This was a small room in which were kept, in addition to normal reference books, past telephone, yellow page, town, and street directories, electoral, rating, and Chamber of Commerce lists, town and country maps, parish histories . . .

The possible identity of E. P. D. T. Glinton proved surprisingly easy to discover. E. P. D. Tourkville lived in Highland Place, East Glinton.

He went along to the detective-sergeant's office, which lay beyond that of the detective-inspector's. Burrow, despite his excess weight, suffered from the cold and since, as always, the central heating had been turned off in April, he had switched on one bar of the electric fire. The small room was airless.

'Our customer could be E. P. D. Tourkville, Highland Place, East Glinton, Sarge. Sounds like a frog. Maybe that's why

12

he's got three christian names.'

Only Noyes, Burrow thought, would find cause for contempt in a man having three christian names.

'So d'you want me to go and question him tomorrow morning?'

'I want you to go now—if you reckon you speak good enough French?'

'*Merde!*' muttered Noyes, who knew that much. He turned.

'Hang on a minute, Pete . . . I'm beginning to think I know the name.' Burrow fingered his lower lip, something he often did when thinking.

Noyes waited, his impatience just about under control. Always over-quick to make up his mind, he'd originally judged the detective-sergeant to be pretty dozy. Time had forced him to revise that harsh opinion. True, Burrow did not have a thrusting, ambitious character, but he did possess a dogged determination, a seemingly endless patience, and an encyclopædic memory, and these could make him a formidable investigator.

Burrow stopped fiddling with his lip. 'Have I ever told you I'm writing a history of crime and the legal system in the county?'

'A couple of times,' replied Noyes, forbearing to add the word hundred.

'I reckon I've come across the name in my researches. And like as not it was in the

13

Peterson book.' He stood, crossed to the glass-fronted bookcase against the left-hand wall, opened the two doors, and visually scanned the top row of books. He picked one out and carried it to his desk, sat, opened it at the index, then at the reference he'd just found. 'Darcy Reinhart Pierre Tourkville was High Sheriff in nineteen hundred and nine.'

'Bully for him.'

Burrow grinned. 'You'll have to mind your manners; you're about to hobnob with one of the leading families.'

'That's all I bloody needed to make my day,' muttered Noyes bitterly.

CHAPTER THREE

Edward Pierre Darcy Tourkville leaned on the top bar of the gate and studied the bullocks which were grazing a new ley. A wonderful bunch and when they'd matured and one of them become Supreme Champion, all the farmers who were forever looking to the Continent for beef breeds could eat humble—or was it umble?—pie.

The light southerly wind flicked at his hair and he reached up to brush a strand away from his forehead. His gaze went past the bullocks and on to the sloping field beyond. The winter wheat was growing strongly and so far—though being prudently superstitious he would never have said so aloud—free of disease. Would that be the last winter wheat he grew? It mostly depended on what new stupidities the Common Market agricultural policy spawned. Ministers were talking about a fresh, realistic, and forward-looking policy, which probably meant things would carry on as before, but dafter. In the referendum on joining the Common Market he'd voted 'No' and nothing had happened since to make him regret his decision even though until recently it was usually agreed that most farming had benefited. If God had intended Britain to have close ties with the Continent, He would not have made her an island. He smiled. If Rosalind, his daughter, heard him say that, she'd know he was mocking himself and would comment accordingly. His smile faded. But David, his son, would probably believe he was being wholly serious and would like as much lecture him on the perils of being a little Englisher. He and David disagreed on so many subjects that it would probably be easier to list those on which they did agree. Some of the saddest rows he and Charlotte had had during the course of their marriage had concerned David; torn between two conflicting loyalties and loves, she had on more than one occasion accused him of being jealous, but this just wasn't true. It wasn't jealousy, but bitter disappointment; and

15

perhaps a sense of guilt because he was so disappointed. And yet when a family had worked and loved the land for generations, wasn't a man entitled to be disappointed when his only son apparently was totally indifferent to the true meaning of such ownership?

At the beginning, indeed throughout almost all his schooldays, David had seemed to be a true Tourkville. He'd loved to walk the fields, to 'look' the animals, to help with the work, to learn the family history. But then he'd begun to question so many of the values the family had always honoured. When Tourkville had complained to Charlotte he'd found little sympathy and she'd told him not to be such an old stick—hadn't the young, throughout history, always questioned the standards of previous generations; after all, hadn't his own brother scorned the land for flying? But questioning had turned into arguing, often with total disregard for feelings. And one day David had declared without any provisos that an estate was no different from any other asset in that it had to be viewed commercially and unemotionally; if the capital it represented could be used more profitably elsewhere, then it must be sold . . . Tourkville had angrily threatened to cut him out of his will so that he wouldn't have the chance to sell the estate; David had coolly replied that he'd never be able to bring

16

himself to do such a thing—even if the terms of the family trust allowed it—because then it would be he who would be responsible for the break with tradition . . .

When David—by now twenty-one and an infrequent visitor—had written to say that he'd been accepted as a research assistant to one of the Liberal MPs, the route by which he had chosen to enter politics, Tourkville had sourly remarked he supposed that that at least was socially preferable, if far less lucrative, to running a brothel. Charlotte had not forgiven him the remark for a long time because it seemed to show a stubborn, pig-headed refusal to accept that his son must lead his own life. But in Tourkville's eyes, politics taught men how to destroy estates, not preserve them . . .

There was a call and he turned to see Charlie waving to him from the far side of the seventeen-acre. At least, he presumed it was Charlie. Without his distance glasses, the figure was just a white blur. He cupped his hands around his mouth, shouted that he was on his way, and began to cross the field. Without realizing it, he walked with careful deliberation, head down so that he could study the land he passed over. One could learn a lot about drainage and fertility just by looking. That was one of the many things that the youngsters, with all their scientific learning, often failed to understand . . .

17

Charlotte said, as he came up to her: 'There's someone wants a word with you, Pierre.'

From the day that she'd first learned his middle Christian name was Pierre, she'd called him by that instead of the Edward or Ted that everyone else used. It was part of her private language, just as Charlie was part of his. 'Who is it?' he asked. 'The man from Black's, trying to sell me more fertilizer than I need? Or the obnoxious young pup from Thorne's who insists I should trade in the combine for a new one?'

'Obnoxious and pup simply because he insisted that the only beef animals economically worth breeding are Charolais or Simmental.'

'The idiot who praises, with enthusiastic tone, all centuries but this, and every cow breed but his own.' He linked his arm with hers and they began to walk towards the tall yew hedge which marked the edge of the house grounds. 'Well, are you going to tell me who he is?'

'A detective-constable.'

'Then I suppose it's to do with my gun licence.'

'No, it isn't; I asked.'

'Then what does he want?'

'He carefully didn't say, which makes it obvious you've been up to something. So confess now, what is that something?'

18

'I've no idea.'

'How very disappointing. I'd been crediting you with all sorts of derring-do.' She released his arm in order to go through the gateway in the barbed-wire fence which kept cattle away from the yew hedge when grazing the field.

He followed her and they walked down the hedge and through the archway into the south-east corner of the large garden. Highland Place, built on the site of a previous house, was basically William and Mary, but in the late eighteenth century an eccentric—or mad, depending on the point of view—Tourkville had decided that the rather severe lines were far too gloomy and had called for extensive alterations and additions, none of which matched each other, let alone the original building. Now, one either dismissed the house as an architectural nightmare or accepted it as an amusing folly.

They reached the turning circle, which enclosed a raised flowerbed, and stepped on to the gravel. 'By the way, I've put him in the library. Ada's doing the green room and says she's determined to finish it before she leaves. I didn't dare disturb her.'

'Since most things seem to disturb her, I'm surprised her husband always manages to look cheerful.'

'No mystery at all. Whenever she gets up steam, he switches off his hearing aid.' They drew level with a parked Escort. 'His name's Noyes, he's young, and prepared to be prickly.'

'But I'm betting that he didn't get that chance with you?'

She smiled, just before she led the way into the huge pedimented porch, thick with Ionic columns.

The library was a large, rectangular room, with a neo-Classical ceiling; the two windows looked out to the west and since the land sloped away there were distant views—on a really clear day, perhaps after rain, it was possible to see a thin line of sea. Bookshelves lined three of the walls and came out on the south one to form two alcoves; all the shelves were filled and the range of books was so great—Tourkvilles added, but never subtracted—that it was impossible to gain from them any judgement on reading tastes.

''Morning,' said Tourkville. 'Sorry to have kept you waiting, but I was down the fields.' He saw a man in the middle twenties with a strongly featured face which even in repose held lines of hard antagonism.

'That's all right, sir.' The 'sir' had obviously been spoken with difficulty.

'Grab a seat and tell me how I can help.'

Noyes settled in the nearer of the large, well-worn leather chairs. He waited until Tourkville was seated behind the large partners desk, then said: 'We've been asked

20

by the Etrington police to help find the next-of-kin of a man who died in an accident on Monday night. Amongst the papers in his flat was one on which were written the letters E P D T and the name Glinton. The only villages in the country of that name are East and West Glinton and the only person with those initials who lives in either of them is you. So did you know a John Harris?'

Tourkville thought for a moment. 'It doesn't ring any immediate bells. We know a Marlon Harris, but he lives in the South of France, so that's not very relevant, is it?'

'No, it isn't.'

Tourkville was amused, rather than annoyed, by this curt dismissal of any small-talk. 'I think it'll be best if I check with my wife before giving you a definite answer—she's a much better memory for names. Is there any reason other than the initials and the name of the village to think I might have known him?'

'None that I've heard.'

'Right, I'll be as quick as I can.'

He left and went through to the hall and across to the green room, which is what they called the smaller of the sitting-rooms even though the predominant colour of the furnishings was now blue. Ada, tall, thin, straight lines rather than curves, was vacuuming one of the carpets. 'Have you seen Mrs Tourkville in the last few minutes?' he asked.

'Ain't seen her since I started in the room.'

He thanked her, withdrew. Ada was moody and quick to take offence, particularly when others could not see any cause, and if a bottle were left within reach she invariably sampled the contents, but she was a careful worker and the only woman in the village willing to do daily work.

He tried the kitchen and sewing-room, then went upstairs to their bedroom. Charlotte was kneeling on the carpet in front of the open bottom drawer of the right-hand one of a pair of beautifully inlaid, bow-fronted, chest-of-drawers. 'Charlie, do we know a John Harris?' he asked.

She sat back on her heels, her lithe, shapely body denying her fifty-eight years. 'I can't think of anyone but Marlon. Why?'

'The man's died in an accident up at Etrington and the police can't find out who's his next-of-kin.'

'What makes them think you could help?'

'Among his papers was an entry, E P D T Glinton. I'm the only person in either Glinton with those initials.'

'Where did you say he was from?'

'Etrington. I seem to remember that that's somewhere near Birmingham.'

She shook her head. 'I'm certain I don't know him . . . Could he have been a salesman who had you marked down as a prospective

22

customer?'

'That's an idea. Perhaps a friend of that young man from Thorne's.'

'Surely you mean that obnoxious young pup?'

When he returned to the library, he found that Noyes, bored by sitting, was standing in front of the fireplace, studying the framed photographs of ships which hung above the carved stone surround. 'I served on them during the war,' Tourkville said. 'Now they look as if they were almost contemporary with the Ark, don't they?'

Noyes turned and his expression was wary, as if he thought he was having his leg pulled. 'You were in the Merchant Service?'

It seemed that Noyes had heard the old dictum: officers and gentlemen for the Royal Navy, men and tramps for the Merchant Service. 'I sailed during the war on refrigerator ships to Australia and New Zealand—two of the most wonderfully hospitable countries in the world. I once calculated that every time we docked in the UK we provided meat, butter, and cheese rations for the population for eight days. And, of course, a small fortune for the stevedores who pinched anything that wasn't bolted down.'

Noyes said impatiently: 'Have you been able to remember John Harris?'

'My wife confirms that we don't know

anyone by that name. But she did suggest that if the initials really are mine perhaps he was a salesman who had me marked down as a prospective customer.'

'He was in his late sixties.'

'Oh! I hadn't realized he was that old.'

'There's no reason why you should. That's all, then. Thanks for your help . . . sir.' This time the pause was long enough to become mocking. 'There's no need to see me out. I remember the way.'

As he watched the detective-constable leave the room, Tourkville decided that the other would always know the way, whatever he was doing.

He turned and walked closer to the fireplace. He stared at the four photographs. It was a long time since he'd really looked at them, even though he was in the library every day; it had taken the detective's vague interest to reopen his mind to them. He wished Noyes had concentrated on something else. Yet again, he decided he would remove them and burn them, even as another part of his brain assured him that he would leave them precisely where they were.

★   ★   ★

Forty-five years ago. A taxi-drive from the marine superintendent's office in Heathfield Street to Gladstone Docks. For part of the

24

journey, they'd travelled parallel with the overhead railway and the high, dirty dock wall. From time to time, he'd caught quick glimpses of masts, funnels, and occasionally superstructure; his excitement had grown. To a young mind, with quick imagination, distant horizons and foreign lands beckoned urgently.

The middle-aged, overweight dock policeman at the gates had noted his brand new uniform, the stiffener still in the cap, and had looked sad. Only later did Tourkville understand the reason for that sadness; so many youngsters set sail, never to return. He'd shown his seaman's identity card and was told the TSS *Waitawea* was at number three.

They'd driven over cobbled roads and crossed train tacks to go between high cargo sheds.

'That's its berth,' the taxi-driver said.

To call a ship 'it' was a solecism of the very worst order. But he'd immediately forgotten that as he caught his first glimpse of foremast and crow's nest, painted in wartime grey . . .

CHAPTER FOUR

He'd been very bitter when he'd learned that because he was the younger son, he could not inherit Highland Place. Not only did it seem totally unfair that one brother should get everything; Daniel was only interested in planes and flying, whereas he felt a mystical attachment with the land. But the laws of primogeniture were sacrosanct; had they not been, Highland Place would never have come down through so many generations of Tourkvilles.

Once he'd accepted the fact, he discovered a love for the sea. Perhaps one of the more disreputable Tourkvilles had been a privateer in the times of the first Elizabeth. Normally, he would have been entered in Dartmouth and from there would have joined the Navy, where he could be expected to do well since his family connections were extensive, he had a pleasant, gregarious nature and a natural ability to lead, and his brain was good but in no way brilliant. But times were not normal. Stock markets had crashed and the Depression had so savaged the countryside that reasonable farmland was fetching only thirty pounds an acre. On top of all this, his father had been one of the dreaming, idealistic, at times naïve Tourkvilles, instead of what was needed, one of the hard-headed, down-to-earth ones . . .

His father had seen himself as the trustee of an ideal rather than of an estate, and so had continued to run it along ancient lines in which service, on either side, was a privilege

26

rather than a duty. But the crisis in agriculture called for sharp business acumen, not idealism. Inevitably, the debts piled up and capital had to be called in . . .

No one, not even his mother who'd viewed him with far greater forgiveness than his wife, had ever been able to understand how he'd convinced himself that he had a flair for finance and that therefore he should handle the investments rather than leaving them in the hands of the family's stockbrokers. After all, he was so unworldly as to believe every word written in a company prospectus on the novel grounds that no one could be such a cad as deliberately to set out to swindle his fellows. By the time he'd learned the fallacy of innocence, half the investments had melted away. So finally he'd had to submit to expert financial and business management. Land was sold off or mortgaged, workers were sacked, and all the hard economies were made which, if made earlier, might have kept the estate intact. One of those economies was to deny the younger son a place at Dartmouth. A loss for which the son was later to find a measure of compensation when he joined the Merchant Navy.

The war, which came to the rescue of farming, also brought salvation to the Merchant Service. Politicians, not being quite so stupid as popular myth would have them, finally realized that if people had to be fed and the country could not produce enough food to do this, then it would have to be imported in British ships. All over the country, in countless backwaters, rusting ships which had swung to their mooring lines and anchors for years, forgotten by all except those who'd once manned them, were hurriedly called back into service. Likewise the seamen. One moment unwanted, the next vital to the country's survival. And soon the politicians, with their natural flair for striking a patriotic note in others, decreed that henceforth the service should be called the Merchant Navy, an honour that would, no doubt, console the men for years of social exile, for being bombed, torpedoed, blasted and burned, for dying with agonizing slowness from thirst, for seeing their escorting vessels retiring and leaving them to the bombers and U-boats on the Murmansk run.

On that overcast, muggy, drizzle-promising day, Tourkville had been an excited, and apprehensive, sixteen-and-a-half-year-old cadet who, as he climbed the gangway, knew that he owed his berth to family connections because the shipping company, of considerable reputation and even more self-appreciation, accepted normally only cadets who'd trained on the Conway or Worcester, or at Pangbourne or Southampton.

28

The chief officer's cabin was on the port side, for'd of the cross-alley. He was a heavily built man, beginning to bald, with a quiet manner. 'Yes?'

'Cadet Tourkville reporting aboard, sir.'

He searched for a scrap of paper, found it, read. 'You're in the after cabin.'

Tourkville waited, but the chief officer resumed work on a cargo plan. He turned away, bewildered, having expected a formal welcome aboard and an introduction at least to his fellow cadets, if not to the other officers.

Eventually, he found the two cadet cabins in the starboard alley, aft of the fourth mate's cabin, for'd of the tenth engineer's. Two bunks one on top of the other, two small wardrobes, a desk, a handbasin, and a settee. The lower bunk had a reefer jacket thrown across it which left him with the upper bunk; instinct told him that this would be the more uncomfortable. He went out and below to the main deck and asked the seaman on the gangway to arrange for his tin trunk to be carried up to his cabin. The seaman told him to bloody arrange the bloody trunk his bloody self. This taught him that a cadet was not an officer.

Once the trunk was in the cabin—a ten-shilling note had secured cooperation—he set out to explore the ship. Some of the facts about her he learned then, some later. Built

29

on the Clyde, she had not been completed until just after the outbreak of war. Of 14,000 tons, she had a cruising speed of seventeen knots. There were six holds, three for'd and three aft; the for'd ones had three 'tween decks, the after ones, two. All decks were insulated except for the upper 'tweens; the middle 'tweens in the three for'd holds had lockers which had been designed to carry chilled beef, but because this took up so much space compared to the telescoped lamb's carcases, none was now carried. Number one and number six each had one pair of derricks, the rest two; winches were electrical and the winch-houses were used as lavatories by the dockers who were too lazy to go ashore. The derricks were rigged to Samson's-posts except for the heavy lift which was rigged to the mainmast; this last had never been used and it was the mate's fervent wish that it never would be because it was a nightmare to set up. The funnel had originally been shorter, but so much muck had blown out over the after deck that it had been heightened by eight feet, leaving it out of proportion. The captain's flat was right for'd on the boat-deck. Aft of the funnel were the wireless cabin and hospital. Since the third officer was the ship's doctor and he could never remember any of the first aid he had been taught by a drunken civilian doctor, it was generally considered to be safer to die

30

than to go into hospital.

War had armed merchant ships. The *Waitawea*, because of her high speed in days when a tramp might have difficulty in maintaining eight knots, was well equipped and she carried twenty-five DEMS ratings and one lieutenant, RNVR, to serve the guns and man the Asdic and radar. For'd, set between the windlass and the hatch coaming of number one, was an eight-foot mounting which carried a dual-purpose three-inch; the bridge and wheelhouse were protected by plastic armour; several inches thick, which was generally held to be a very good thing because it was from there that the FAC's and PAM's were fired—rockets, trailing wires with bombs on the end, designed to blast attacking aeroplanes out of the sky, credibly credited with having damaged several of the ships which had summoned up the courage to fire them; on each wing of the bridge was a raised, circular mounting which carried a twenty-millimetre Oerlikon; on either side of the boat-deck were two more mountings; in the for'd one another Oerlikon, in the after, twin Browning .500's; right aft on the main deck was a six-inch and above and for'd of this a multiple rocket launcher, fired by an operator who prudently sat in a steel shelter . . .

★   ★   ★

'They talk about a brown study; I reckon you've been away in a black one.'

He jerked his head round and saw Charlotte was standing in the doorway of the library.

'I heard the detective drive off and called out to ask you if he'd said anything more, but answer came there none. When I called again and there was still silence, I began to be worried.'

One day, he thought, one of them would call and the other would be unable to answer then, or ever again . . .

'Why are you looking like that?'

'Someone's walking over my grave.'

'Then tell them to get the hell off it.' She came forward. 'Is something wrong, Pierre?'

He shook his head.

'You're looking as if . . . as if you've just heard some very bad news.'

'I haven't heard anything.'

'Then why so grim?'

He answered reluctantly. 'I was remembering.'

'Remembering what?'

'The old *Waitawea*.' He looked across at the right-hand photograph—a poor one because he had had to take it hurriedly and surreptitiously since photographing ships had been illegal during the war.

'Remembering what about her?' she asked,

32

wondering if she could finally persuade him to tell her the full story.

'That she was the unhappiest ship in the company.'

'Why was that?'

'Because of the Old Man. He went out of his way to make all of our lives, but mine in particular, hell. Looking back on things, he must have been suffering from some kind of shell-shock. His previous ship had been bombed from under him.'

'Didn't the officers try to compensate for the way he behaved?'

'It's not all that easy; in any case, they didn't try. The mate was only interested in a quiet life so he wasn't going to do anything which might upset the Old Man, the second loved himself and nobody else, the third was a natural bully, and the fourth was a weak fool.'

'They sound horrible.'

'To a cadet on his first voyage, they were. To someone slightly more mature, I suspect they'd merely have appeared pathetic or ridiculous.'

'And when the ship was torpedoed?'

'Forget it,' he said, his voice suddenly harsh.

Right from when she'd first met him, he had been loath to talk about what had happened; for the past year or so, the memories had seemed to haunt him even

33

harder, but he'd still kept them to himself. Yet she was certain that if only he'd talk about them, he'd find some degree of relief. She sighed.

CHAPTER FIVE

Noyes parked in the large courtyard at the back of Divisional HQ. As he walked towards the main building, the detective-sergeant came out, saw him, and crossed.

'Have you seen Tourkville yet?' Burrow asked, as he came to a halt. He hurriedly tucked his hands into the pockets of the brown parka he was wearing because the wind was cool.

'I'm just back.'

'Then I hope you remembered to touch your forelock as you said goodbye?'

'Bloody funny.'

'You know, Pete, you ought to try to see the funny side of things.'

'Some things don't have a funny side . . . He doesn't know a John Harris. But he does know a Marlon Harris who resides in the South of France, if that's of any help.'

'Immeasurably . . . He's no suggestions as to how his initials came to be on that sheet of paper?'

'His only idea is that the dead man was a

34

commercial traveller who had him listed as a prospective customer.'

'When Harris was in his late sixties?'

'He wouldn't know much about the lives of such people, would he?' Noyes carefully forgot that Tourkville had originally had no idea of Harris's age.

'I don't suppose so . . . I've been giving the case the odd thought. Like I said earlier, it's difficult to think that a man in Tourkville's position would have anything to do with Harris. Yet if he didn't, it's one large coincidence about the initials . . . And as far as Harris is concerned, who these days can live without personal papers as he seemed to be doing—cheque-book, plastic money, pension book, and all the rest?'

'It's not our case, so who the hell cares?'

'You've a point there. So let Etrington know we can't help and they'll have to sort our their own problems. By the way, was he frightfully huntin', shootin', and fishin'?'

'Just condescending.'

'And the missus? For my money, the missus is usually the worst. Real snooty bitches.'

Noyes didn't answer.

Burrow looked curiously at him, nodded, and walked on.

Noyes crossed to the main building and went inside, climbed the stairs to the third floor and CID quarters. In the general room

35

there was one of the other DC's and he had a brief chat before sitting at his desk and typing out the message to be Telexed to Etrington.

He took the message down to the secretaries' room where four civilian women worked and fended off the heavy-handed advances of the more concupiscent members of the force, then left, to try and obtain another witness statement.

It was well after eight that night when he arrived home. Home was a semi-detached, in a road of semi-detacheds, with a very small front garden and a larger back one. The asking price had been considerably more than the limit they'd set themselves, but Carol had liked it so much she'd persuaded him to buy it. Since its value had risen considerably, it had proved to be a very good investment. Normally, he took pride in this possession, but now he compared it to Highland Place. He cursed the rich who destroyed so much for so many.

Carol was in the kitchen. Almost as tall as he, she maintained a slim, fashionable figure without recourse to dieting. Light brown hair, whose natural curl was occasionally augmented at the hairdresser's, framed a face that was by some standards a shade too long; very blue eyes, high cheekbones, and a Roman nose, incorrectly suggested some foreign ancestry. When she smiled, her face softened and a couple of years slipped away.

Possessing a natural flair for clothes and being able to buy them cheaply from the shop, she dressed with considerable chic.

He crossed to where she stood, by the gas stove. ''Evening, love,' he said. He kissed her and then for once deemed it politic to apologize. 'Sorry I'm a bit late.'

'You admit that it is a bit late?' she asked curiously. 'You really do realize it's too late to go out as we'd decided, so I've had to lash together a meal?'

'I got called out to a job at the very last moment.'

She stirred the contents of a saucepan with a wooden spoon. 'And no doubt went uncomplaining?'

He knew a familiar flush of bitterness; why couldn't she understand that his job was not one where tomorrow was as good as today? 'It wouldn't have done any good to shout my head off—I was the only DC in sight. And finally I had to wait at the bus stop for over a quarter of an hour for a sixteen.'

'Frustrating.'

'Well, you had the car.'

'I'm very sorry. In future I'll bus, you take the car.'

'For God's sake . . . Look, I never gave a definite time for getting back. I just said I'd try to make it in good time.'

'And this is what you call good time?'

'No it isn't; I said it wasn't.'

'Then you didn't manage to do what you said you would; doubly frustrating.' She used an oven cloth to bring out a casserole and half a dozen baked potatoes, each wrapped in foil. 'Are you completely worn out by your frustrations, or could you manage to get two plates?'

He opened the cupboard door with too much force and it crashed back on the refrigerator.

'It doesn't matter,' she said sweetly, 'I'll get them.'

'The door slipped out of my fingers.' He put two plates on the table.

'Help yourself to stew. And would you like three or four potatoes?'

'Four. With butter.' She was trying to persuade him to cut his consumption of animal fats. 'And salt.' She was also trying to make him eat less salt.

'That does remind me. When we go out to a meal, Pete, it would look better if you could not add salt until you've tasted the food. Otherwise, it's being rather rude to the cook.'

'If you're thinking of the other night at Ruth's, that's not a bad idea. It might just get it through to her that it's too much salt in the cooking which is bad; none at all and nothing tastes of anything.' He spooned some stew on to his plate, added four potatoes, went over to the small eating area and put the plate down. He opened the refrigerator door and searched

38

for the butter.

'I'm surprised you dislike Ruth so much.'

'It's her cooking I object to.'

She might not have heard him. 'After all, she is so much your type.'

'Yeah?' He carried the butter dish over to the table and sat. 'So tell me what is my type?'

'Frothy and full of.'

'Full of what?

'Availability.'

'Bloody funny.' As he cut open the potatoes and generously buttered and salted them, he remembered the detective-sergeant's telling him that he ought to try to see the funny side of things. He wished he could. Then this bitchy conversation might never have started; and even if it had, it wouldn't have reached its present stage. Yet the real trouble was not any lack of a sense of humour, but his inability not to accept a challenge and fight back.

'Still, I don't think I need lose too much sleep over her,' she continued, as she helped herself to stew and the two remaining potatoes. 'After all, as far as you're concerned she doesn't possess the ultimate sex symbol.'

'Is that right?'

'Her hair's bottle blonde, not red.'

Back to Judy.

★   ★   ★

The new mortuary was in south Etrington, a hundred yards from the river Blane. The building was styled like a house and it was set in its own grounds; council gardeners kept the lawns cut and the beds tidy and indulged in black humour whenever an undertaker's van drove into the covered parking space.

The PM room was kept as clinically clean as a hospital surgery and two large extractor fans kept the air constantly changed when the centrally placed examination bed was in use; even so, there was always a faint, pervasive smell which initially tightened the stomach of anyone who, from experience, knew its origin.

The pathologist, a Scot who after forty years in the South still spoke with as strong an accent as when he'd left Invergordon, worked with quick skill. His assistant stood close by, ready to hand him fresh instruments, but the other men present stood well clear and, except for his secretary, concentrated their minds, as far as possible, on other things.

'Very interesting!' said the pathologist, as he peered closely at the dead man's throat.

The DC brought his mind back to the immediate present and reluctantly looked at the corpse. 'Is there something you didn't expect, sir?'

'The superior cornu of the thyroid has

40

suffered a fracture.'

The DC tried, and failed, to remember something, anything, about the thyroid.

'So now we see if there's any bruising under the skin; there's none apparent on it.' He asked for the table to be adjusted slightly and his assistant worked the controls; the dead man's head rose slightly and tilted to the left. The pathologist resumed work with a very fine scalpel.

Several minutes later, he straightened up, handed the scalpel to his assistant, eased his back. 'Strangled manually.'

'It definitely wasn't the fall which killed him?'

'Not only is the superior cornu fractured, there are also bruises under the skin, indicating the points at which the finger pressure was applied.'

★   ★   ★

The detective-inspector was relatively young for his rank; ambitious, clever, hard-working, he had every reason to believe that he would attain high rank sooner rather than later. 'We're dealing with a murder, not an accident?'

'That's right, sir,' replied the detective-sergeant. 'Could be that the killer made Harris tight, throttled him, and pushed him over the balcony, hoping death would be attributed to the drunken fall. The lab boys are checking his alcohol consumption.'

'Have his dabs gone off for checking?'

'Sent them myself, half an hour ago.'

'D'you expect them to be recognized?'

The DS thought about his answer because if it was considered sloppy the DI, too sharp for anybody else's good, would jump down his throat. 'I'd say there's a fair chance, sir. There's a bit of a look to him.' To a layman, that would have seemed the very epitome of a sloppy answer, certain to arouse the scornful wrath of the DI; but to a fellow detective it made sharp sense. The criminal and the policeman, the hunted and the hunter, learned to identify each other in life by signs that the ordinary person would miss—and unusual watchfulness was perhaps the most common of these. Sometimes such signs seemed to linger on into death, as the image of the murderer was once believed to remain in the murdered man's eyes. The DS waited, but there was no comment. 'On top of that, he was unusually anonymous. We've hardly been able to learn a thing about him.'

'Why not?'

'None of the papers we found give us any sort of a lead.'

'But it's ten to one he was drawing the OAP.'

'I've had a word with the pension people and they say he's not on their books.'

'No medical card?'

'None and he's not on any of the local surgeries' lists.'

'Banks, savings accounts, credit card companies?'

'All negative.'

'Only a Buddhist monk can live in this world without money. How did he pay for the flat?'

'Fifty thousand in cash.'

The DI fiddled with a pencil. The honest man usually never handled anything like that sort of sum in cash, but as always there were exceptions so that this fact on its own proved little. 'Was it bought through agents and which solicitors handled the work?'

'There were no agents involved. The previous owner advertised in the local rag and Harris turned up, had a look round, and settled for the asking price. Thrushby and Feagan had always acted for the seller and, at Harris's request, did the same for him. They told me they were surprised by the payment being in cash, but as the chap I spoke to said, there's nowt so queer as folks and it's perfectly legal.'

'How did he live from day to day? Was there much money in the flat?'

'A few quid in a wallet, but not enough to buy the main course at the Regency,' the DS answered, naming the most luxurious of the local restaurants.

43

'Did he run a car?'

'No . . . Incidentally, the caretaker confirmed that he entertained a succession of young men.'

'Which will have cost him.' The DI dropped the pencil on the desk. 'How well was the flat searched?'

The DS spoke carefully. 'Well enough for an accidental death, probably not for a murder.'

'Done at half-cock? Then you'd better get back there and personally make certain it's searched sufficiently well for any eventuality, hadn't you?'

'Yes, sir.'

★   ★   ★

In the second bedroom of the flat, a small wall safe was found behind a framed Lipton print which seethed with violent colour but no form. It was locked and there was no sign of the key. The name of the maker of the safe was telephoned through to a firm of specialist locksmiths in the next town and they promised to send a man immediately.

The safe was opened early that evening. It contained just over ten thousand pounds in notes of varying denominations.

'Now just what in the hell was his racket?' said the DS as he finished counting the money and, a uniform PC acting as witness, sealed it up in large, stout envelopes, which he initialled and then passed to the PC to do the same.

CHAPTER SIX

Tourkville stared at the figures and wished they weren't quite so unambiguous. The downturn in farm income was hurting, as it was most other farmers, but what was financially rocking the boat was the cost of the overdraft, by far the largest part of which represented the purchase price of Dower Farm. He'd known at the time that the farm, put up for auction, would probably be expensive—two of the adjoining farmers had also coveted it—but he had not expected the price to go quite so high. Not that it had mattered then, because the bank manager had previously intimated that if necessary the agreed overdraft limit could be exceeded. But what neither of them had foreseen had been the abrupt agricultural depression, a result of EEC policies, and the subsequent, heavy drop in land values. Now the manager was asking for an immediate reduction in the overdraft, implementing the promise originally made to repay at regular intervals . . .

He looked up and through the nearer window at an oak tree which stood in the far corner of the garden. Family history had it that Gwain, who'd naturally chosen the losing side in the Civil War—no Tourkville could ever be a Republican—had planted the acorn when a boy of five and twenty-three years later had been shot within the young tree's shade by a vengeful detachment of Roundheads when he had refused to betray a friend. It might have been possible to test the validity of this story, but no Tourkville had ever dared do so for fear that it might turn out to be merely legend. It was only right that the past should be a history of service, honour, and self-sacrifice . . . The present, unfortunately, was usually far less heroic. He'd accepted at the time that the purchase of Dower Farm could not be warranted in business terms—his accountant had made that clear—but it had been a part of the estate which his father had been forced to sell . . .

Charlotte entered the library and when she saw his expression she said with sudden concern: 'What's wrong, Pierre?'

'Nothing.'

'Dear man, do you really think I could be married to you for umpteen years and not know when something's the matter?'

'I was just thinking.'

She approached the desk and identified the papers spread out on it. 'The bank's making noises?'

'The manager says he's got head office on

46

his back.'

'He's a wimp. But quite apart from that, why's head office suddenly become belligerent?'

'It's their money.'

'All right. Then take a leaf out of the South Americans' book and borrow more and more until you owe them so much that they daren't get nasty.'

'I shouldn't have bought Dower Farm.'

'Fiddlesticks! That was one of the happiest days of your life. You're to stop worrying because my stars say it's going to be a good week for me and my family and I always believe them when they're optimistic . . . I originally came in to say that Rosalind's phoned. She wants to bring a friend down for the weekend a little later on.'

'Male?'

'Yes, hence the formality of giving us so much warning. She hopes that by the time they turn up, you'll have reconciled yourself to his appearance.'

'You're not telling me he's one of these punks?'

She laughed. 'Do you imagine that even she would have the nerve to bring one of those here? She's not talking about his looks, just using a figure of speech. She's trying hard to ensure that this visit doesn't turn out to be as disastrous as the last one.'

'Depends what he's really like, doesn't it?'

47

'You've got to admit, you did make your feelings plain. But then I suppose it was rather stupid of him to lecture you on the evils of possessions.'

'Left-wing loony . . . How the hell does she find them?'

'Probably in a similar fashion to the way in which you used to find your bits of fluff when you were young and experimenting.'

'I did not look for bits of fluff and I did not experiment.'

She came forward and kissed him on the cheek. 'You're irresistible when you become pompous.'

'Thank you for those few kind words.'

'Clamber off your dignity and smile.' She settled on the edge of the desk. 'Rosalind asked me especially to tell you that she's certain you'll like Mike because he's fascinated by old things.'

'There's a double-edged comment, if ever I've heard one.'

'Of course. She is your daughter, so never misses the chance of a friendly dig.'

'It's funny how . . .' He stopped.

'What were you going to say?'

'How different she is from David.'

'That's normal.'

'But she's such a sense of humour.'

'And so has David, if only you'll approach it from the right angle . . . Pierre, I do wish you'd try to get on better with him.'

48

'Has all the effort to be made by me?'

'No, of course not. But he is rather serious about some things and you really ought to accept that and not needle him; and anyway, you can't expect the young to be flexible. They're so certain they're always right and it takes time for them to discover they aren't.'

'By which time it's often too late.'

She was surprised by the sudden note of harshness in his voice. 'Too late for what?'

'To save the estate.'

'For God's sake, you're surely not still holding what he said against him, are you? I'm quite certain he was only trying to annoy you. When he inherits, which I hope to heaven won't be for years and years, he'll guard everything just as fiercely as you.'

'Perhaps. And if it's still there to be guarded.'

She looked at the papers on the desk. 'It's not like you to get so pessimistic . . . Is there something more wrong; something you haven't told me about?'

He made an effort to speak lightly once more. 'Have I ever been able to keep a secret from you?'

'Not for very long,' she replied complacently. She slid off the desk. 'I suppose I'd better go and start the lunch. And since all those figures are making you morbid, lock them away and go out and tramp the fields.' She started to walk towards

49

the door, came to a stop. 'I knew there was something else I wanted to tell you. I was reading the hatches and dispatches in the paper and Adrian Young has just died. How long have Anne and Phil had to put up with him—ten years? And for the last two or three he's been quite impossible. I'll write, of course, but I don't know whether to make the letter one of commiseration or congratulation.' She continued on to the doorway and left the library.

Young. A name to remember. But not Adrian Young; Captain Young, fiftyish, five feet two inches tall when standing very upright, a face fashioned out of badly hewn rock . . . The voyage which was to end with tragedy started with farce.

They'd left the docks at high tide, cast off the two tugs, and sailed up the buoyed channel to join the other thirty-four merchant ships and eight escorts of the convoy. It was a day of gusting wind, frequently reaching force six, and quick, fierce showers.

The captain, on the starboard wing of the bridge, gave the order: 'Hoist signal letters.' The third officer, standing by the engine-room telegraphs, gave the order: 'Hoist signal letters.'

The words meant nothing to Tourkville and he looked to his fellow cadet, Stevens, for enlightenment. It immediately became clear that in spite of three years on the *Worcester*,

Stevens was just as mystified as he. Not knowing what to do, they did nothing.

The captain became aware that his order had not been carried out. 'Third, didn't you hear me?' he asked harshly. 'Hoist the signal letters.'

The third left the telegraphs and stepped over to where the two cadets stood. 'Hoist the bloody letters.'

'But, sir . . .'

The captain gave a string of helm and engine orders to line the *Waitawea* up on her position in the outside starboard column and the third had to race back to the telegraphs.

As soon as the manœuvre was completed, the captain turned and looked up at the signal yard; when he saw that none of the halyards carried a hoist his face reddened, his cheeks puffed, and he shouted. It was the first time that Tourkville realized the expression, wild with rage, could occasionally be taken literally. The captain began to sound hysterical.

The third cowered before the tirade; then, when it came to an end, he turned on the cadets and verbally assaulted them. Finally, he reluctantly and blasphemously explained that the signal letters were a four-flag hoist which identified the ship, to be found in the flag locker.

Hoisting a flag on a balmy summer's day was one thing; hoisting a four-flag hoist in a

51

cold, heavily gusting wind was something else. The rope tried to pluck itself free and seared the flesh of their palms, the flags billowed this way and that and eventually wrapped themselves around a funnel stay and could only be persuaded to unwind after many panicky seconds . . . But eventually they raised the hoist.

A destroyer came abeam of them and her large signalling lamp began to flash.

'What's he want?' demanded the captain angrily—he hated the Royal Navy.

The third, who had picked up the Aldis lamp, replied: 'I'm just getting the message, sir,' as he failed for the third time to read a word. The signaller aboard the destroyer, no doubt with tired resignation, flashed even more slowly.

'Well?'

'He's asking what ship, sir.'

'What ship? What ship? What ship does he think we are? Tell the bloody fool to read our hoist.'

The third, not quite so stupid as to relay the question literally, worked the trigger of the lamp. The reply was prompt. 'You are not on our guest list, *Aewatiaw*. Are you sure you're invited?'

The captain, who had no sense of humour, gave it as his considered opinion that with the Royal Navy on their side they had no hope of winning the war. Then he swung round, almost losing his cap to the wind as he did so, and stared aloft. For a moment he could say nothing and his face just grew steadily redder, like some African primate posteriorly declaring its love, then he began to scream with uncontrollable fury. The four flags had been hoisted upside down. In truth, it had briefly occurred to Tourkville to wonder why the top flag had only reached within two feet of the sheave.

Ninety seconds later, the hoist was the right way up.

The destroyer flashed again. 'Welcome to the party. Have the first round on me.'

★   ★   ★

For some reason never explained, the captain blamed only Tourkville for the humiliating episode of the upside-down hoist; Stevens's equal responsibility was forgotten. Made even more vindictive than normal by the belief that the whole of the hated Navy were now laughing at him, the captain set out to harass and humiliate Tourkville at every opportunity. The officers could have shielded the cadet from some of this vindictiveness, but they were either too self-centred or too weak to do so.

In the North Atlantic, where the danger of being attacked was held to be greatest, double watches were kept; this meant four hours on watch, four hours off, except for the dog watches; these last ensured that the hours actually kept in each twenty-four alternated. In the twelve hours off watch, officers and cadets had to sleep, eat, wash, take sights, and carry out any other duties which were theirs by virtue of rank or were allocated to them. For those who had reached maturity, double watches were unwelcome, but for the cadets, young, still immature, used to and requiring long and uninterrupted sleep, the outside limit of roughly only three and a half hours' sleep at any one stretch became a form of torture. Their minds wreathed in cotton wool, the pain fierce behind their eyes, they would fall asleep as they paced the bridge, to be awoken painfully as they crashed into the dodgers or rails.

On the sixth day out, a day of heavy squalls, moderate to rough sea which kept the ship pitching, and a strong wind which lashed the spray against the crated aircraft on the hatch squares, a phone buzzed in the wheelhouse. Tourkville heard it, but did not move.

'Answer it,' snapped the third, suddenly bad-tempered because the captain was with the second on the leeward wing which meant that he had to stay on the exposed windward one.

Tourkville tried to make sense of the words.

'Answer the bloody phone.'

He finally cleared his brain sufficiently to understand the order. He went round the plastic armour screen and into the wheelhouse; once inside, his sleep-starved mind forgot what it was he had come to do.

The zigzag clock buzzed and the helmsman visually checked with the board and then put on ten degrees of port helm. 'Have you lost something, then?' he asked mockingly, as he watched the gyro repeater. Sharp, intelligent, Andrews, an ordinary seaman, knew how to impress a strong officer or take the mickey out of a weak one without ever becoming guilty of loggable insolence. He treated cadets with amused condescension.

Tourkville stared uncomprehendingly at Andrews.

The second, prismatic station-keeper in his right hand, hurried into the wheelhouse. He checked himself when he saw Tourkville. 'Up two,' he said, before returning to the wing.

Tourkville did not move.

'Hadn't you better tell 'em, then?' said Andrews.

'What?'

Andrews grinned.

The captain had a voice which carried. They heard him demand to know why the distance between themselves and the next ship was still increasing and what alteration in revs had the second last made. The second's answer was inaudible.

The captain entered the wheelhouse, his lopsided sou'wester making him look like a very bad-tempered gnome. 'Have you told the engine-room.'

There was a buzz. Tourkville stared at the bank of telephones on the starboard bulkhead beyond the wheel.

'Answer it, boy.'

He walked over and picked up the receiver under a flashing light. He heard the steady roar of the engine-room and a man's voice. The words made no sense. Thickly, he asked the engineer to repeat the message. He was given some figures which he promptly forgot.

'What do they want?' demanded the captain.

He was too dully bewildered to try to answer.

'Third. Third.'

The third ran in from the port wing.

'What's wrong with this boy?'

'I don't know, sir.'

'What's the engine-room want?'

'I don't know, sir.'

'Is there a single bloody thing you do know?'

'But sir, I've been out on the wing . . .'

'Don't just stand there. Find out what in the hell's going on.'

The third phoned the engine-room, spoke briefly, replaced the receiver. 'They've been trying to report the revs and sea temperature for the last watch, sir.'

'Have they put the revs up two?'

'They didn't say, sir.'

'Then why didn't you ask?'

Resentfully, the third phoned back to the engine-room. He reported. 'Their last order, sir, was down two.'

The captain lost his temper. He referred to his officers as the biggest bunch of incompetent landlubbers this side of the Royal Navy . . . He stopped as he noticed that Tourkville was now leaning against the bulkhead, his eyes shut, rocking gently to the ship's movements. 'He's asleep!' he screamed. 'The bloody boy's asleep on watch!'

The third grabbed Tourkville's shoulder and shook violently. Tourkville jerked awake.

'You were asleep on watch! Actually asleep on watch!' None of them would have been surprised if the captain had begun to foam. He swung round to face the third. 'Tell the chief that this boy's to work on deck this afternoon to see if that'll teach him to stay awake on watch.'

Sleep lost. It was a viciously cruel order.

CHAPTER SEVEN

A telephone rang in Etrington CID general room and one of the older DCs answered it. He reported to the detective-sergeant. 'Dabs have just come through on the Harris case. His real name was John Harwood and he had form.'

'I thought he had! What's his history?'

'Records are sending the file on, but the outline goes like this. Born in Manchester, father cleared out, mother a bit of a slag. In minor trouble when a kid. Went to sea during the war and was off our books for a few years, but eventually turned up on penny jobs. Done three stretches, the last one four years back.'

The DS leaned back in his chair. 'So how come that he finally lived it up in style, with over ten thou in the safe?'

The DC grinned. 'I wouldn't know, but if ever you find out the answer, let me into the secret.'

★   ★   ★

Noyes ate quickly, knowing that he'd have to leave the house soon if he were to reach the station on time. Carol came into the kitchen. 'D'you want some more coffee?'

'No, thanks.' She was wearing a gaily patterned frock with a flared skirt and he thought she was looking a million dollars.

'I may be late this evening.'

He could not prevent himself asking: 'Why?'

'Because.'

He accepted that his question, antagonistically put, had been a mistake, but he was not prepared to back down now. 'Because what?'

'Because I may be.' She looked directly at him. 'If you can be late without giving any reason, so can I.'

'That's different.'

'How?'

'It just is.'

'When will you ever realize that you can't set up two standards and you can't ride roughshod over other people?'

'What's all that supposed to mean?'

'That you ought to have learned by now that what's sauce for the gander is just as much sauce for the goose and fighting doesn't prove anything.'

'You're talking daft.'

'You think you aren't fighting me now? Then look in the mirror in the hall and see how far out you're sticking that thick, square chin of yours.'

'Don't be so ridiculous.'

'Afraid of what you might see?'

'No.'

'I suppose that's true enough. You've never learned to be afraid, not even of yourself.'

'Why in the hell are you talking like this?'

'I suppose because I'm getting so tired of having to fight back.'

'Then don't.'

'And earn your contempt?'

'I just don't understand you.'

'I know. And that makes me so sad that I don't know whether to cry or empty a can of cold baked beans over your head.'

At any other time he might eventually have smiled, but now he just continued to stare angrily at her.

She said dully: 'So I'll see you tonight when I see you.'

'You are reckoning on coming back, then?'

'Would you rather I didn't?'

He made no answer.

'You're tempted?'

'I wish to God you'd think straight.'

'But above all, submissively?'

He ate the last of the toast, stood.

'I hope you have a good day,' she said.

As he walked through to the hall and picked up his mackintosh, he wondered whether her last few words had been a form of peace offering or had been intended ironically.

He left the house and walked along to the bus stop, in Ebor Crescent, hardly aware that the morning was sunny and an optimist would have spoken of summer. She'd accused him of always fighting, but she was no slouch at that herself. And she knew his weaknesses and how to wound him. Why had she refused to explain why she might be late? Was it because she believed he was knocking around with Judy and she was saying that she was going to start looking around? If so, then he might as well set out to prove that her suspicions were justified . . .

The first bus was a sixteen and it dropped him a quarter of a mile from Divisional HQ. He'd been working at his desk for ten minutes when the detective-sergeant called him along to his room.

''Morning, Pete. Weather's more like it, isn't it? Another few days of this and that new rose of mine will be out.'

'Hoist the flags.'

'Bit of a heavy night, eh?' Burrow grinned. 'Or you just don't go for roses?'

'I've nothing against 'em if someone else does the growing.'

'Do you good to go in for gardening; make you cool down . . . Pull a chair up and have a butcher's at this.'

As Noyes read through the report from Etrington, Burrow brought a pipe and tobacco pouch from his pocket and slowly and carefully packed the bowl with tobacco.

Noyes looked up. 'So how did he make

enough cabbage to buy a fifty thousand quid flat and have ten thousand more in a wall safe?'

'It's a good question, when you remember that his record says he was never anything more than a small-time crook.' Burrow lit the pipe.

'If they were any good up in Etrington, they'd have found some answers by now.'

'From their report, they've not been idle.'

'But they've got nowhere, so now they want us to do their job for them.'

'Same as you would in their position.' Burrow tamped the burning tobacco with the base of the lighter. 'I expect you've noticed something interesting?' He was only an occasional, and therefore fussy, pipe-smoker and he often spent more time in fiddling than smoking. 'Harwood was at sea. Didn't you tell me Tourkville had been at sea when he was a youngster?'

'Yeah.'

'So there is one thing that they have in common; maybe there's more.'

'Between the landed gentry and a back-street thief?'

'Stranger things have happened.'

'If you'd spent any time with Tourkville, you wouldn't think so.'

'All the same, you'd better go back and ask him if he recognizes the name of Harwood.'

*   *   *

Noyes slowed the CID Escort as he approached Highland Place along the gravel drive. Despite himself, he enjoyed the sight of the ancient, architectural hotch-potch of a house, set amid velvet lawns; even though it didn't belong to him, it gave him a sense of belonging.

He parked by the side of the raised, circular flowerbed, crossed the drive, went into the grandiose porch and pulled the fox's head; inside, a bell rang.

Ada opened the door and she studied him with her sharp, buttony, brown eyes. 'Yes?'

'I'd like to speak to Mr Tourkville.'

'You can't.'

'My name's Detective-Constable Noyes . . .'

'Don't matter if it's Prince Charles, you still can't.'

'Why not?'

'Because he ain't here,' she replied with deep satisfaction.

'Where is he?'

'Ain't none of my business. Ain't none of yours, no more.'

He was about to disagree heatedly when there was a call from inside. She turned, listened, then answered: 'He says he's from the police.' Her tone suggested that she was quite prepared to discover he was a liar.

63

'Wants to speak to Mr Tourkville.' She listened again, then turned back. 'She says you can come in.'

He entered the hall.

'Good morning, Mr Noyes,' said Charlotte.

He was surprised she remembered his name.

'It's nice to see you again.'

She had actually sounded as if she meant that. He was even further surprised to note the apron she wore over her frock; Carol would never have dreamed of wearing an apron when she went to the front door.

'I gather you'd like a word with my husband. I'm sorry, but he's out at the moment. Is there any way I can help?'

'Not really.'

'No substitutes! . . . Well, he did say that if he could get away before lunch he'd be back around twelve, but if he couldn't, he wouldn't make it before the middle of the afternoon. Would you like to come in and wait a bit to see which it is?'

He looked across at the inlaid grandfather clock, with painted face, that was ticking contentedly to the right of a full set of mounted armour. 'If that's all right with you?'

'Yes, of course. And maybe you'd like some coffee while you wait?'

'Thanks.'

She turned and spoke to Ada, who was too

interested in what was going on to have returned to work. 'Would you be kind enough to make some coffee? We'll have it in the green room.'

'If you say.'

Noyes was impressed by the green room, not so much by its size—it was not as large as the library which he'd seen on his previous visit—but by the way in which elegant furniture and furnishings made it a room of quiet beauty. There were half a dozen framed portraits in oils hanging on the walls, executed at different periods, and as he stared at them, annoyed because he was impressed, he reminded himself that while they'd been living the life of Reilly, the poor sods working the land had had to struggle even to feed themselves.

'Some of my husband's ancestors,' she said. 'The trouble with them is that they all look so smug and righteous. I've always wished we'd a painting of Bainbridge Tourkville to add to them—he was a younger son and when he died at the age of twenty-seven he had the reputation of being the biggest rake in the country. I can't help feeling that he'd alter their expressions for the better.'

He was astonished that she should speak of them in such irreverent tones.

'Do sit down, Mr Noyes. I don't know about you, but I always find just standing so very tiring.'

65

He sat.

'Do you live in Watlingham?'

'In west Watlingham.'

'That's a nice part of town. Especially near the park. It always makes such a difference in a town to have some open space. Don't you agree?'

'Yes.'

She seemed not to notice his antagonistic reserve, but continued to chat with easy friendliness. Before long, he began to respond. On learning that he was interested in sailing, she said how, when she and her husband had been younger, they'd had a small yacht on the coast and had often sailed across to France. She asked him what kind of boats he'd sailed and whether he enjoyed racing and he told her of his ambition, very seldom expressed, to crew in the Fastnet . . .

Ada entered, carrying a tray on which were silver coffee-pot, milk jug, and sugar bowl, and two cups and saucers. She put the tray down and left, not prepared to hand round the cups.

Later, the carriage clock on one of the display cabinets chimed once. 'Half past,' said Charlotte, automatically looking at her wristwatch to confirm her words. 'I'm very sorry but it does seem that my husband won't be returning until well on this afternoon.'

'Then I'd better be getting back.' He stood.

'I'm sorry you've had a wasted journey. Is there any message I can give him?'

'If you'd tell him I'll be along some other time.'

'I imagine you're here because of that poor man who died in Etrington?'

'Yes. We now know it wasn't an accident, he was murdered.'

'Oh dear, how terrible. It really has become a violent age, hasn't it?' she said sadly.

It had always been, he thought, but in the old days the likes of her had largely been insulated from the violence.

'But I think my husband told you that he'd never met the poor man?'

'That's right. But there's something more we now know—his real name was John Harwood. It's just possible that Mr Tourkville will recognize that. So like I said, I'll be along soon to find out.'

CHAPTER EIGHT

Tourkville arrived home at six-thirty and Charlotte met him in the hall. 'How did it go?' she asked.

'I need at least half a dozen gin and tonics.'

'Really as bad as all that?'

'Worse. The in-fighting was so savage that the only reason the room wasn't knee deep in gore was because their veins are filled with acid.'

'I wonder what it is about animal clubs that makes people so vicious?'

'Their human egos. I threatened to suspend the meeting if they didn't return to the agenda.'

'With what result?'

'They turned on me instead of attacking each other.'

She laughed. 'The way of the peacemaker has always been thorny . . . Let's go through and you can have the first of your many gins.'

They went into the green room and he crossed to the cocktail cabinet, so beautifully made that it complemented the antique furniture instead of competing with it. 'What's yours?' he asked.

'I'll have the same as you, please.'

'Ice?'

'Not for me. But if you're still boiling, I'll get you some.'

'There's no need; the steam's stopped coming out of my ears.' He opened the cabinet and poured out two drinks. 'Has anything happened on the farm front?'

'The vet came and had a look at the two bullocks which Fred was fussing about. He doesn't think it's anything worse than a touch of anæmia.'

'Why the devil should they be suffering from that?'

'That's what Fred asked. He'd no idea.'

'Which won't stop him charging an exorbitant fee . . . What's the treatment?'

'Iron and liver injections. The iron ones are a bit tricky because some animals can react badly to them.'

'Then one of the two will.'

'Nonsense. Think positive and optimistic, as the man on the television said last night.'

'Blithering idiot.' He passed her a glass. 'Nothing else?'

'George had a spot of trouble with the sprayer, but he soon got it working again.'

'He's by way of being quite a mechanic. Bit of a difference from Thompson.'

'Careful, or it'll look as if you're counting your blessings rather than your disasters.'

He sat and stretched out his legs. 'I'll swear that Laura's father was a turkey-cock. When she started on about breed standards, all those double chins swelled and she gobbled.'

'How she'd be hurt to hear you talk like that. She thinks you're a charming, old-fashioned gentleman.'

'How would you know?'

'She told me so, the last summer show.'

'I don't believe a word of it. She couldn't be that pleasant if she tried.'

'You've no idea of the charm you pack . . . Which reminds me: your charm doesn't always work. The detective called again this morning and he was still trying to be prickly.'

'What's he want this time?'

'To say that the man he was asking you about didn't die in an accident, he was murdered.'

'You'd have thought they'd have found that out before now. But why bother to come here and say so?'

'To ask if you know him under his real name, which was . . . Damn!'

'No, I don't know anyone called that.'

'Don't be stupid. Just for the moment the name's gone, but I'm sure it had something to do with furniture.'

'Escritoire? Commode?'

'Much more Anglo-Saxon . . . Harwood, that's it. John Harwood.' She happened to be looking at him and she saw the sudden expression on his face. 'You do know him, then?'

'Maybe.'

'Who was he?'

'A steward on the *Waitawea* and one of the survivors was called John Harwood.'

There was a silence which she broke. 'Then if the dead man was he, probably those were your initials he'd written down?'

'No,' he said harshly.

'But since you knew each other . . .'

'Forget it.' He finished his drink, stood, went over to the cocktail cabinet and poured himself another.

She was frightened.

70

                    *   *   *

He sat in the library and stared out at the
darkness beyond the window whose curtains
were not drawn. John Harwood, alias Gert.

Gert and Daisy. A couple of poofters, as
they were called in those days. Gert slightly
the younger, slim, darkly handsome in a
smoothed-down, self-conscious style,
affected; but for Daisy, he'd have been
cruelly mocked by most of the crew. Daisy
was built like a tank and if fairly slow to take
offence, because it sometimes took him time
to realize that offence was intended, his anger
was to be feared. Before the ship had sailed
on her last voyage, a man in a pub in Dock
Street had jeered at Gert in unambiguous
terms. Daisy had beaten up the man with
heedless violence.

In the *Waitawea*, the officers' saloon was at
the for'd end of the accommodation,
immediately below the officers' smoke-room.
Aft of the saloon, on the port side, was a
small pantry in which the food, brought from
the galley, was kept warm until required.
Daisy worked in the pantry, Gert served at
table.

There were three tables, the central one of
which was longest by four feet. Tradition,
and the company prided itself on its
traditions, dictated who should sit at the

71

captain's table—an honour that some would cheerfully have forgone—and where. Naturally, the central table was his and he sat at the head; on his right was the chief officer, on his left the chief engineer (oil and water never mixed, so of the ten engineers, three electrical engineers, and three refrigerator engineers, only the chief was permitted to eat in the officers' saloon); beyond the chief officer, the second officer, beyond the chief engineer, the chief radio operator; and then, since this was wartime and in spite of the captain's hatred of the Royal Navy, beyond the chief radio operator, the RNVR lieutenant. Only one of the other two tables were normally used, by the third and fourth officers, second and third radio operators, and the cadets; company tradition did not lay down their places. At sea, neither of the tables were ever fully occupied.

Once through the Panama Canal and into the Pacific, normal watches were kept. Tourkville was on the 4.0 to 8.0. This meant he should have been relieved by Stevens for dinner at seven, but on the fourth day out Stevens did not arrive on the bridge until seven minutes past. He did not explain his tardiness, but strongly advised Tourkville to skip the fish because it tasted as bad as it smelled. Tourkville left the bridge and did not bother to have a quick wash in the cabin because now he'd only twenty minutes in which to eat his meal. The fourth was at his table, but no one else, the others all having eaten at the earlier setting.

Gert came and stood by his chair. 'Are you having the soup?' he asked in his soft, syrupy voice.

He read the menu. Tomato soup, fried plaice, beef and Yorkshire pudding, sultana roll, cheese. There was no rationing at sea. 'Yes, please.'

The fourth officer made no attempt to be sociable; newly promoted, after obtaining his second mate's ticket, he did not possess that sense of natural authority which would have allowed him to mix freely with a junior while in his own eyes retaining the standing of his rank.

Gert, his hands beautifully manicured, served the soup. Tourkville began to eat.

'Boy!'

He put his spoon down in the soup and looked up. The captain and chief engineer had remained behind, the captain talking, the chief engineer resignedly listening. The captain was glaring at him. 'Boy, where have you just come from?'

Since the captain knew he'd just been relieved, it was a ridiculous question; but one did not inform a captain of that fact.

'Have you lost your tongue?'

'No, sir.'

'Then answer.'

'The bridge, sir.'

'I see.' In the tropics, the captain was the only officer who did not wear open shirt and shorts; he favoured collar and tie and starched jacket, together with long trousers—he looked somewhat Edwardian. He fidgeted with his tie. 'And on your way down from the bridge, did you have the elementary manners to wash and tidy yourself before entering the dining saloon?'

For a few seconds Tourkville remained baffled and then he remembered something—just after one bell, the fourth had told him to go up to the monkey island and check the gyro repeater. While up there, he'd stumbled and had fallen against the wooden and canvas dodger and this had left a smear of sooty dirt across the front of his shirt. He'd meant to change the shirt before coming down to the saloon, but Stevens's late relief had made him forget . . .

'Well?'

'No, sir.'

'Why not?'

'I was in a hurry to come down here, sir, because I was late.'

'Why were you late?'

To have explained that Stevens had relieved him seven minutes after he should would have been to land him in the mire. 'I don't know, sir.'

'There seems to be a very great deal you do

74

not know, not least of which is the degree of manners expected of an officer.'

He could think of nothing useful to say in reply to that except that all his experience so far suggested that a cadet was only *mutatis mutandis* an officer.

'Since you lack the manners expected of an officer, it will clearly be more fitting if you cease to dine with them . . . Steward.'

Gert hurried across.

'You will move the boy's place to the third table. In future, he will eat all his meals there.'

Even the chief officer showed his astonishment at the fact that a man of the captain's age and rank should have issued so childish and vindictive an order.

Gert crossed to where Tourkville still sat. 'You go over and I'll move everything.'

Tourkville sat at the third table. Gert put the plate of soup, cutlery, and glass of water in front of him. 'I'll get your roll and butter now.' He leaned forward. 'Stupid old bastard.'

★   ★   ★

All meals at sea were of necessity served in two sittings, the first for those off watch, the second for those newly relieved. Tourkville, who together with the chief and fourth officers would relieve the third now on watch, went down to the first sitting of breakfast. The officers watched with brief interest as he went over to the third table, the cadets, when satisfied they were unobserved, gestured derisively. He felt very much alone.

Gert placed a pot of coffee and a milk jug on the table. 'Porridge, haddock, bacon and eggs?'

'Yes, please.'

'Could you manage three eggs?'

As always, four hours on the bridge had sharpened his appetite. 'I could.'

'And a couple of extra rashers of bacon?'

He suddenly became worried. Why this sudden generosity? Did it signal an unwelcome redirection of Gert's affections, following a row with Daisy? His concern was very short-lived. 'Thought you'd like to know,' Gert whispered, 'we both spat in the silly bastard's porridge to learn him.' It became clear that it was sympathy, not passion, which beat in Gert's bosom.

After Gert had left, Tourkville stared with fascinated expectation at the captain, who sat ramrod straight at the head of the central table. But he appeared to be quite unaffected by the culinary ordeal through which he was, unknowingly, passing.

★   ★   ★

From then until the day the ship was

torpedoed, Gert made certain that Tourkville dined like Lucullus. When there was steak, his was the largest and juiciest; when others had two slices of roast lamb, he had four; if cream (it wasn't real cream; no one wanted to guess what it might be) was served with tinned peaches, his peaches were invisible beneath it; if he wanted a second helping of steam duff, he was always given it, even when the other cadets were told there was none left. As Stevens said bitterly, what the hell was the point of washing?

★   ★   ★

As Noyes drove up to Highland Place on Saturday morning, through the sun and shadow caused by puffball clouds and a light easterly wind, he saw Charlotte kneeling on a pad on the central, raised flowerbed. He was surprised she should be weeding; he'd imagined that the rich always got someone else to do their dirty work for them.

She stood as he stepped out of the car. 'Good morning.'

''Morning, Mrs Tourkville.' She might be an old girl, he thought, but she had a young girl's smile. She must have been quite a smasher when young.

'I'm glad to say you haven't had a wasted journey this time!' She moved to the edge of the bed. 'He's over in Flannel Field, trying to decide whether to plant a vineyard this winter.'

'A vineyard?'

She stepped down on to the drive. 'They're becoming quite the thing these days, especially with milk and maybe grain quotas making life so difficult for everyone. According to the experts, they're the most profitable crop of all, but that makes me rather wary. My father used to say that the two quickest ways of going bankrupt were borrowing money and listening to experts.'

He smiled.

'But I have to admit that the idea has its attractions. For a start, how does the name Château Highland sound for the wine?'

'I think I'd expect a malt whisky.'

'That's probably right. Then perhaps Château Tourkville? The French flavour certainly wouldn't do any harm. But my husband would probably say that it would be self-advertising . . . In any case, on the analogy of the chicken and the egg, perhaps we shouldn't worry about a name until the wine's in the barrel. But you don't want to stand there listening to me waffling, you want to speak to my husband. Have you boots or wellingtons with you?'

'Yes, in the car.'

'Then you can go across the fields—if you wait here for him to return, you could be all morning. As any farmer's wife will tell you, it's very important that a farmer should lean on a gate and look . . . Do you see that ash?'

He looked across a field to the right and saw a pollard ash, whose main trunk was huge and partially hollow.

'Just to the right is a gate. Go through and diagonally across the field and in the left-hand corner you'll find another gate. The field beyond is down to barley, so go round the edge. Flannel Field is the next one on.'

'It sounds as if you've a lot of land?'

She said, a touch of amusement in her voice: 'We do own several hundred acres, yes. And you think that's wrong?'

He had tried to keep his tone neutral, but had obviously failed. He was surprised she should challenge him, having placed her as someone who would not welcome direct confrontation. 'Why should I?'

'A lot of people do; people who don't understand.'

'Don't understand what?'

'That owning land creates a trust; it's not like owning a block of shares which you can do what you like with. Sometimes it can be more of a burden than an asset.'

There were some burdens a man would like to have the chance to shoulder.

'It's never as easy as the other person believes.'

'I reckon not much is, Mrs Tourkville.'

'Perhaps . . . When my husband inherited

the estate, because his elder brother had earlier been killed in the desert, some of the land had been sold, a lot of what remained was still mortgaged, the buildings needed repairs, the stock was of poor quality . . . For the first years, he worked himself into the ground. Eventually, he began to sort things out and then we joined the Common Market. Good news for some farmers, but bad news for others. But if I start talking about their agricultural policies, I'll use language that'll shock you!'

He grinned.

'You should do that more often . . . Forgive me, but I've reached the age where I'm allowed to make remarks that if I were younger would be considered unpardonably rude.'

He wondered exactly why she thought he should smile more often?

'I must return indoors and do some housework; it's terrible when one runs out of excuses for not doing it . . . So if you make your way to Flannel Field, you'll find my husband. And do you happen to know anything about frost lines?'

'Not a thing.'

'A pity. He's trying to work out how far down the field the vines could be planted with safety. Tell him to bring you back to the house for a drink, won't you?'

'That's very kind of you, but I'll have to

get straight back.'

'What a pity. Then I'll say goodbye now.'

He changed into wellingtons and walked half way up the drive before turning off and crossing to the ash tree. He did not immediately open the gate to the right, but stared out across the gently sloping land. How far did the estate stretch? To the lane? Or beyond and up to the super pylons? Quite something to look out and know that it all belonged to you; to be able to walk and walk and still own the land . . . Angrily, he checked his thoughts. Quite something for the owner. But what was it for the poor sod who couldn't even afford a few square feet of suburban garden?

Tourkville was at the end of the field.

''Morning,' Noyes said.

Tourkville nodded.

'I imagine your wife told you I called yesterday?'

'Yes, she did.'

'And she explained what I wanted?'

'To ask if I knew the man whose real name was Harwood, not Harris.'

'Did you?'

'I didn't.'

'He was at sea during the war.'

'Perhaps. So were countless others.'

'I just wondered if your paths could have crossed.'

'Not to my knowledge.'

81

'Did your wife add that it wasn't an accident, he was murdered?'

'Yes.'

'This makes the investigation a very much more serious one.'

'I imagine it does.'

'So remembering that, are you quite certain you never met him?'

'Remembering that can't alter the facts.'

'I wasn't suggesting it could.'

Tourkville stared out over the land, seemingly losing interest in what was being said. Noyes felt he was being dismissed with lordly disdain. 'Then I don't need to bother you any more.'

'Sorry I can't help.'

And up yours, he thought, as he left.

★   ★   ★

Charlotte was arranging flowers in a large Waterford vase in the green room when Tourkville entered. 'Good. I was just about to try and call you to say lunch was almost ready . . . Linda rang a while back and we're asked to dinner on Tuesday to meet the Ramseys.'

'Are they the couple whom Linda keeps saying are so charming and intelligent?'

'That's right.'

'So we'd better expect uncouth Neanderthal.'

'What on earth's got into you?'

82

'Worry at the thought of meeting someone Linda extols.'

'But I thought you liked her?'

'I do. It's her judgements of other people I doubt.'

She looked at him for several seconds before picking up a deep purple rose and carefully positioning it in the vase. 'What did the detective say when you told him you'd been at sea with Harwood?'

'Nothing.'

'I take it, you did tell him?'

'As a matter of fact, I didn't.'

'Why ever not?'

'Because from the day we landed in the UK after being picked up, I've not clapped eyes on him and so even if those were my initials he'd written down, I've no idea why.'

'But if the police . . .'

'Tell them that I'd sailed with Harwood and they'd never stop asking questions.'

'Why should they, once you'd explained you knew nothing about him?'

'Because they're never content with a negative. In no time flat, their heads would be full of crazy ideas.'

'What sort of crazy ideas?'

'That I knew something about why he was murdered.'

'Which you don't?'

'Of course I damn well don't. Not a goddamn thing.'

83

She usually knew when he was lying and he was lying now.

★   ★   ★

Burrow was in the CID general room, talking to one of the other DCs. He turned as Noyes entered. 'Well?'

'I've seen his lordship.'

Burrow chuckled. 'From the sound of things, he didn't push out the boat?'

'Stuck-up bastard.' Noyes reached his desk and slumped down in the chair. 'What makes him think he's better than anyone else?'

'Position, money, education, all those funny little things.' Burrow's tone changed. 'Come on, snap out of it. If you had a million in the bank you'd still be poor by Getty standards, so would you hate him just because of that?'

'Why not?'

'Because that's what's known as being bloody daft. Did Tourkville recognize Harwood under his real name?'

'No.'

'You said he'd been at sea?'

'Yeah. And in that distant, superior voice of his, Mr Tourkville informed me that so had countless other men.'

'When all's said and done, that's fair comment.'

'Your sense of fairness makes me want to

84

heave.'

Burrow shrugged his shoulders. Sometimes a chip on the shoulder grew so heavy it became a log that couldn't be moved. 'Then you can tell Etrington that we've done all we can and there's no joy.'

CHAPTER NINE

Noyes looked at his watch. 'I suppose I might as well get moving.' He pushed his empty glass across the bar.

'So long, then,' said the barman as he picked up the glass. 'And if the Gunners ain't thrashed, I'll take up knitting.'

'You'd better buy some needles.'

As Noyes walked across to the outer door, he wondered what had happened to Sid, the nark he was supposed to have met there. He hoped it was nothing serious. Sid was useful.

He stepped out on to the pavement and turned left.

'Am I invisible or have you got a date with a blonde?'

He swung round and came face to face with Judy. 'Two blondes and a brunette.'

'There's a man who's a glutton for pleasure.'

'Some pleasure comes better in quantity.'

'Never mind the quality? . . . Been boozing

on your own?'

'That's right.'

'Dangerous.'

'That's what makes it fun.'

'So now find out how much more fun it is with me.'

He hesitated.

She linked her arm with his. 'I've met dead men more eager than you.' She moved forward and he, perforce, had to accompany her.

When they entered the bar, the three men looked at Judy with interest, the only woman with critical dislike.

'D'you remember what I like?' asked Judy. 'I mean, when it comes to drinking.'

'Port and lime.'

'Right. What a performance!' She crossed the floor to sit at a corner table.

He went up to the bar; the bartender winked and said: 'Beats football any day of the week.' He ordered a port and lime and a Scotch and as he waited he stared at Judy's reflection in the large mirror behind the bar. Despite the fact that the capital H of Haig, written across the centre of the mirror, obscured a third of her, the remaining two-thirds vibrated. One didn't wonder if, but how. Yet he was certain she wasn't an easy lay. The obvious ones often weren't. She'd given him the come-on, but only because he hadn't. She wanted to be fought

86

for. Woo her without fighting and she'd offer only scorn. She was supposed to have a husband, but if she had once, there was no sign of him now. Perhaps his fate had been like that of the male praying mantis; consumed at the moment of consummation.

He carried the glasses over to the table.

'I've a bone to pick with you,' she said. 'I've been waiting and waiting for a phone call.'

'Yeah?'

'Couldn't find the change, I suppose?'

'How d'you guess?'

'Maybe you didn't look very hard?'

'That could be right as well.'

She stared smoulderingly at him over the rim of the glass. 'Has anyone ever told you that you're a bit of a bastard?'

'Lots of women, lots of times.'

'I was on my way home to cook supper.'

'So drink up and then you won't be delayed.'

'Are you hungry?

'I'm on a diet.

'I'm very good at home cooking. Come and try.'

'*Pas ce soir, Joséphine.*'

'That's for me to say. I'm not saying it.'

'Wouldn't make much sense if you did.'

She brushed back from her forehead a curling strand of luxuriant red hair. 'Shall I tell you something, Peter Noyes? There are one hell of a lot of men who'd jump a mile at the chance of that invitation.'

'Then invite them all along and have yourself a private Olympics.'

She drank. She ran her tongue carefully along her very full lips. 'When you're ready, it's on me. I mean, the other half.'

'Not for me, thanks.'

'In a rush?'

'That's right.'

'For your home cooking?

'Right again.'

'A man with only one desire.'

They left the pub and came to a stop on the pavement. 'How are you getting back?' she asked.

'By bus.'

'Then you go that way and I go this . . . Unless you'd like to change your mind and we both go this way?'

'See you around, maybe.'

She laughed knowingly. 'You'll see me around, certain.'

They parted and he walked along to the bus stop. When a number eight came along, he boarded and went up on to the top deck and along to the right-hand front seat. He stared out at the road ahead, imagining what might have been. Why had he rejected the invitation? Because of Carol? He'd not so far betrayed their marriage—a fact that would have surprised many—but their rows had become so frequent and so bitter that it was difficult to believe there could be much life left in it. Betray it now and he'd probably not be destroying something that would otherwise survive. Or was it because he had instinctively judged that despite all that Judy had said and inferred, he needed to reject her a little longer if he were to attain success and not end up as one more male praying mantis?

The bus stopped at the top of Clovis Avenue. He walked down to the crossroads and then along to Grassington Crescent. Carol's greeting was warmer than it had been for some time. 'Guess who phoned half an hour ago?'

'The Queen of Sheba.'

'Ever hopeful . . . Maggie.'

'Maggie Simonds?'

'She and Tim have just returned to this country and are staying with her mother until they find a flat for a short rent. She wants us to go and see them as soon as possible. When can we?'

'I might be able to slide off early tomorrow if the DI's in a good mood.'

'Do you realize we haven't seen them since we were married?'

'Hardly surprising since they went out to Zambia or Zetland or wherever.'

'I don't think geography can be your strong point.'

'I once placed Vladivostok south-west of

Moscow. The geography teacher congratulated me for not trying South America.'

'I like generous people.' She came up to him and put her hands behind his neck. 'Do you remember how cheerful Maggie got on our wedding day?

'Cheerful? Pie-eyed.'

'Tim kept trying to get her to drink black coffee and all she could do was ask for more booze . . . Why are you looking like that? Scared that because I'm remembering our wedding day I'm about to become all sentimental?'

'Why should that worry me?'

'Because great big he-men get uneasy in the face of sentimentality.'

'Who says?

'Well, don't you?

'Try me.'

'I think you're confusing sentimentality with lust.'

'Why not?'

'Why not indeed?' she said and then kissed him.

★   ★   ★

The first day of June was warm and sunny and that evening the BBC weatherman smiled; he was quite excited when he said that Friday was expected to be equally sunny and even warmer.

Tourkville entered the house through one of the three back doorways and changed out of his wellingtons into slippers in the game larder. Charlotte was in the green room and she used the remote control to switch off the television set. 'You've just missed the nature programme and there's nothing worth looking at now until quite late . . . How's the expectant mum with complications?'

'Finally produced a nice-looking bull calf and as far as we can tell, none the worse for it. Fred's got green fingers where stock's concerned.'

'Surely a bit of an Irishism?—but I know what you mean. He told me not so long ago that when he was young he wanted to be a vet, but there just wasn't the money to see him through the course.'

'A pity—he'd have made a damned good one of the old kind, who thought more of the animals than the latest theories and techniques.' He settled in one of the armchairs.

They heard a shot.

'That was close,' he said. 'And who the hell's shooting at this time of the night?'

There was a second shot. 'That's down at the pond!' He quickly came to his feet.

'What are you going to do?'

'What d'you think? Find out who the hell it is.'

'Take Fred or George with you.'

'Fred's out with his wife as soon as he's cleaned up and George and his wife are away, seeing their son and daughter-in-law.'

'Pierre, I'd rather you didn't go on your own.'

'I'm sorry, but I'm not going to stay here and just listen to someone blazing off at the duck.'

'But I've an awful feeling.'

'After the last one, the washer in the downstairs cloakroom gave out. Have a spanner ready for when I get back.'

'I wish you wouldn't sometimes treat me as a fool.'

'Never as a fool. Just as someone who has five premonitions before breakfast and who remembers the one that once proved to have some slight foundation of fact and forgets all the rest.'

There was a third shot. He hurried over to the door.

'At least let me ring the police and tell them what's happening?'

'Whoever's doing the shooting will be in the next county by the time they get here.'

In the game room were several ash sticks, cut over the years, and he chose the heaviest. Outside, the sky was clear and the moon was entering its second quarter and there was sufficient light for him to make his way across the fields without needing to switch on the torch he'd picked up before leaving the house.

There was a fourth shot and he saw the flash. He turned right, to make a wider sweep which would bring him immediately behind the point from which the shot had come. Damned ignorant vandal, he thought. The shooting season for duck didn't open until September. Any true poacher observed the seasons.

The pond had always been there, but several years previously he'd brought in a dragline and had had the pond enlarged and, in parts, deepened; that done, he'd planted trees round it. It had proved to be a very successful flight pond, especially with a dozen or so pinioned mallard put out as decoys. Then, for no particular reason, certainly not from any disgust of the past, he'd lost any desire to shoot and had turned to conservation. So now it was a flight and breeding pond in which mallard, teal, widgeon, and the occasional shelduck enjoyed security. Security, that was, except from poachers. He reversed the stick so that the heavy head was free to strike. He'd have no compunction about hitting any man who shot at duck in June.

The trees, in full leaf, loomed higher against the starry sky and he came to a stop to listen. Judging from that last shot, the poacher should now be immediately ahead of

93

him, inside the belt of trees which at this point was roughly forty feet deep. Far away, a vixen gave her agonized love call; nearer, an owl hooted; nearer still, a nightingale, no longer disturbed by the shooting, resumed singing. But there was no sound of human movement.

A duck suddenly took to the air amidst a flurry of wings, feet, and water. Probably, he judged, it had sat tight earlier, but had then finally taken fright as the poacher drew very close; that put the poacher to the right. He moved right, came to a halt fifty feet on. Silence. He entered the belt of trees.

Ten feet inside, his right foot caught in a bramble trail and he stumbled, but managed to move his feet quickly enough not to fall; instinctively, he had let go of the stick and torch and they crashed into the brambles with considerable noise.

There was a shot and a spear of flame, close enough to shock him for several seconds. Then, as his normal sense returned, he heard the noise of someone running away.

He found the stick and torch and left the trees. No running figure was visible in the moonlight. Very aware of an inner tightness, the aftermath of tension, he began to walk back to the house.

CHAPTER TEN

Burrow looked up as Noyes entered his office. ''Morning.' He waited until Noyes was seated in front of the desk, then said: 'Last night, around nine-thirty, Tourkville was in his house when he heard shooting by a pond. He went out to find who it was. The pond's surrounded by trees and as he moved into them he tripped up on some brambles, almost fell, and kicked up a bit of a row. A gun went off pretty close to.'

'But it missed him? Bad markmanship.'

'Don't talk so bloody daft,' snapped Burrow, for once showing sharp anger.

'All I was saying was . . .'

'Let's get something straight. It doesn't matter what your politics are, just so long as you leave 'em at home. If you're soft enough to dislike a man simply because he's more than you have, that's your privilege when you're not at work. When you are, it doesn't matter if he lights his fags with fifty-quid notes, you don't like or dislike him. Got it?'

'Yes,' answered Noyes sullenly.

Burrow reached into the pocket of his sports jacket and brought out his pipe. 'Tourkville rang the local copper and PC Franklin went along. Franklin reports that Tourkville reckons the shot was either an accidental one or a warning not to move any closer; his wife, on the other hand, is convinced the poacher was aiming at him.'

'She was with him?'

'No.'

'Then she can't judge.'

'That's right. Unless Tourkville has told her something he didn't mention to Franklin.'

'You're suggesting it could have been an attempted murder; that the first shots were to draw him to the pond?'

Burrow lit his pipe. 'Commercial poachers, the gangs from towns, are getting rougher, but I wouldn't say that attempted murder has become their style yet. And they don't usually operate in June, when it's that much more difficult to sell the stuff because it's out of season.'

'Did Mrs Tourkville suggest why anyone should set out to murder him?'

'No. Franklin put it all down to mild hysteria—a wife's reactions to the thought of her husband being shot. But I've been wondering. After all, Tourkville could have a connection with a murder—Harwood's—and that might well provide the motive here.'

'He denies ever having known Harwood.'

'I'm not forgetting. But he could be lying. And if that was attempted murder at the pond, then it's odds on that he is.'

'Which brings us round to the original

96

question.'

'Yeah. So suppose you go and have another word with him?'

'And get the same answer as before, but with a thicker coating of ice?'

'Then start off by tackling things the other way round. See if you can discover anything which suggests that it was attempted murder and not an amateur poacher either giving a warning or suffering a loose trigger finger.'

'How am I supposed to go about doing that?'

'You'll think of something.'

'I'm thinking lots of things . . . I've enough work on my plate for five, skipper, and the Harwood case isn't our pigeon.'

'But an attempted murder of Tourkville is.'

*   *   *

George Weight led the way across the field to the belt of trees around the pond. In his middle to late thirties, he had a limp, the result of a tractor accident when much younger, which only became apparent when he hurried. 'It's near to the blasted oak—over to the left.'

They entered the trees and passed an oak which had been struck by lightning some years before, losing part of it's trunk in a vertical line. Weight came to a stop. 'According to what Mr Tourkville says, it's somewhere about here.'

Noyes looked about him, then went forward to the water's edge. There seemed to be birds everywhere, adult drakes in their full plumage, ducks and youngsters in drab browns. 'I suppose he murders the bloody lot of 'em a bit later on in the year?' he said with contempt.

'Doesn't shoot no more,' replied Weight equably. 'This is a sanctuary.'

Noyes's temper was not improved by this answer, which destroyed any mental pictures of privileged slaughter. 'D'you reckon there'll be traces of poaching?'

'Could be if he didn't know what he was doing. Feathers, a crippled bird or two.'

'I wouldn't know if they're crippled or doing the three minute mile. Can you see any?'

Weight, with a countryman's quiet contempt for the ignorance of townspeople stared out at the birds on the water. 'Can't see none, but like as not they'd be hiding up.'

'Then how about having a bit of a search around?'

Weight walked slowly off, weaving his way between trees. Noyes returned to the spot at which it was probable that Tourkville had been standing and searched the ground all around. The soil was sufficiently moist where bare of undergrowth to record impressions, although without any clarity. After a while, he reckoned he could pinpoint where Tourkville had stumbled and was reasonably certain that someone had been standing some thirty feet away, almost at the water's edge. There was no empty cartridge case near the latter position, but ten feet to the right—not really in the direction in which Tourkville had been—there was an ash tree and marks on this suggested puncturing by pellets. He had a penknife with him and tried to dig out a pellet from the trunk, but it was obvious that he would need a far stouter stool.

He began to walk round the edge of the pond and was struck by the strange fact that although the duck were in constant, and at times phrenetic, movement, the scene as a whole was one of peaceful beauty. Timeless was a word that came to mind. He remembered Charlotte Tourkville's telling him that the ownership of land was a trust, which brought responsibilities, sometimes onerous. Reluctantly, he accepted that he was beginning to gain some idea of what she'd meant.

Because he and Weight had been walking round the pond in the same direction, they did not meet until Noyes had reached the spot from where they'd started. 'D'you find anything?' he asked.

'There was a couple of birds what could be pricked, but they was strong enough to swim away so there's no knowing for sure.'

'What about feathers?'

'Plenty of them, but nothing special.'

'I thought you said you'd be able to tell?'

'I said maybe. Sometimes shooting takes out a load of feathers which couldn't have come naturally, sometimes it don't.'

'And this time it didn't?'

'That's right.'

'It looks like there are some pellets in a tree and I need to dig a few out—have you anything that'll do the job?'

'Up in the workshop, aye.'

'Let's go and get it.'

They began to walk up the field, down to paddock grazing, so that the varying height of the grass, and consequently the depth of its greenness, created a chequerboard pattern.

'What's it like working here?' asked Noyes.

'Near the same as working most places,' replied Weight.

'Have you been here long?'

'A few months.'

'Then there's a bit of a turnover of staff?'

'There always is when someone pinches.'

'Like that, was it? . . . How d'you find his royal highness?'

'D'you mean, Mr Tourkville?' asked Weight, quietly correcting Noyes's brashness. 'There's worse.'

Noyes had been hoping to hear that Tourkville was a bastard of an employer.

*   *   *

Jenkins, the detective-inspector, was beginning to run to fat. His hair was rapidly thinning and he grew it long on top to try to hide this fact. His face was heavily lined, especially about the mouth, which made him look older than forty-one. He'd once been ambitious, now he was content if things ran smoothly. 'It's all very insubstantial, to say the least.'

'I know, sir,' said Burrow. They had a good working relationship, each content to accept the fact that the other was, if perfectly competent, no ball of fire.

'But if Etrington should come up with a definite and meaningful connection between Harwood and Tourkville, we could be made to look pretty slack for not having got to it first.'

'That's the way I see it.'

'Have we heard anything yet on the pellets Noyes retrieved from the tree?'

'Only that they're size five.'

'What's that mean?'

'It's a reasonable size for duck.'

'So that doesn't take us anywhere?'

'Not really.'

'You know, I've met Tourkville a couple of times—not that he'd remember. He seemed a nice enough bloke, of the old school. It's difficult to think of there being any sort of a

101

connection between him and a petty crook.'

'In the normal course of events, yes. But they have been together at sea.'

'Suppose they were—does that suggest a motive for Tourkville's murdering Harwood?'

'No. But if they were together, why does Tourkville go on and on denying the fact?'

'Seems to me that you're spending a lot of imagination on bringing facts together which may have nothing to do with each other, then basing a premise on them . . .' He fiddled with the tip of his prominent nose. 'There must be a way of finding out if they ever were at sea together. Do we know which concern Tourkville was with?'

'The Far Eastern Pacific and Australasian Steamship Company.'

'That's a mouthful.'

'Maybe it's like funnels used to be—the more a ship had, the better and faster the passengers thought it.'

'Is that right? . . . I think we'd better follow the matter up a bit further. If we find Tourkville did know Harwood, then there'll be some questions need answering.'

★   ★   ★

Tourkville was loading bales of hay on to a sledge behind the smaller of their tractors when he saw Charlotte, accompanied by a man, walking across the field. Glad to take a rest—he was a lot fitter than many sixty-year-olds, but a well packed bale of hay now made him grunt—he stopped the tractor's engine.

'This is Detective-Sergeant Burrow,' she said.

He shook hands.

'Sorry to stop work like this, sir,' said Burrow, using the word 'sir' naturally and without any hint of the resentment there would have been in Noyes's voice.

'Then don't be. I'm grateful for the break.'

'Can't you pack it in?' asked Charlotte.

'With a sky like that?'

She looked up. Clouds were rolling in from the east and their black edges presaged rain. 'How many more bales are there to carry?'

'Just over a hundred. And Fred will be along to help at any moment.'

'I won't keep you,' said Burrow. 'All I've come to ask is, what were the names of the ships you were on?'

Tourkville's manner changed. 'Why d'you want to know that?'

'If it was an attempt to shoot you, we're wondering if the motive could somehow be tied up with your time at sea.'

'I've said more than once that nobody tried to kill me, it was an ordinary, ignorant town poacher.'

'We can't be certain of that.'

'I'm telling you.'

'Pierre . . .' began Charlotte, then stopped.

Burrow seemed unconcerned by the sharp, antagonistic note there had been in Tourkville's voice. 'You're probably right, sir, but it's our job to check whether maybe it wasn't quite as simple as you think. So if you would give me the names of the ships?'

'I was at sea forty-five years ago.'

'Yes, I do have a note of that.'

'That's a hell of a long time ago. There can't be any connection.'

'You know, it's funny how things can tie in sometimes.'

In the face of such unfailing good humour, it was difficult for Tourkville to do anything other than answer: '*Waitawea, Wopotiki, Togotapo, Maurangi.*'

'That sounds rather like someone swearing in Hindustani! Can you spell those names for me?' He wrote them down, closed his notebook and replaced this in his pocket. 'That's all, then; thanks a lot. And just in case things aren't quite like you think they are, Mr Tourkville, I'd be a bit careful—if there's any more trouble, call us out rather than doing anything yourself.'

'Don't worry,' said Charlotte, 'the next time, I ring immediately.'

'That's fine. I'll say goodbye now and leave you to get on with your work.'

For a while they watched him cross the field, then Tourkville turned. 'I'll load the

104

rest of the bales.'

'No,' she said sharply.

'It looks like rain . . .'

'I don't give a damn if it buckets down and they all float away. I must know.'

'Know what?'

'Why you won't admit to them that you sailed with Harwood on the *Waitawea*.'

'There's no reason as far as they're concerned other than that it can't be of the slightest consequence to them.'

'Someone tries to kill you and you say it's not of any consequence? Why are you being so stupid?'

'Nobody tried to kill me. Either the gun went off by accident or he was telling me not to get too close.'

She was about to say something more when she saw Doyle enter the field.

'Best get movin', with the look of the weather,' said Doyle as he reached them.

'Fred, could you get in the rest of the bales on your own?' she asked. 'Mr Tourkville's not feeling a hundred per cent and I think he ought to rest.'

'That's no problem.'

'It's very kind of you.'

Tourkville followed her across the field. When the tractor-engine started, making it certain they couldn't be overheard, he said: 'Why am I now suffering from a diplomatic illness?'

'Because I'm going to discover once and for all why you'll never talk about what happened at sea and why you've been frightened of something for the past months.'

'Nothing's been frightening me.'

She walked on, her face set in stony lines, bitterly hurt that he would not voluntarily tell her the truth.

CHAPTER ELEVEN

Ada was in the kitchen, wearing a flower print frock whose lines made her appear even more angular than usual. 'I've done the dining-room.'

'Thank you,' said Charlotte.

'The stain behind the radiator's coming through again and there ain't nothing more I can do about it. You'll have to get it replastered, or something.'

'All right.'

Ada stared at her. 'Is something wrong?'

'Just a bit of a headache.'

'Then you'd best lie down,' Ada looked accusingly at Tourkville, blaming him for not being more responsive to his wife's suffering. 'D'you want me to stay on a bit?'

'No, thanks. I'll be fine.'

'You see she rests,' Ada ordered Tourkville. She picked up her handbag and rolled-up plastic mackintosh and marched out of the kitchen.

'You've talked us both into being invalids,' said Tourkville.

She did not respond to his attempt to speak lightly. 'Let's go through to the other room.' She led the way up the short passage, across the hall, and into the green room. 'Will you give me a whisky, please?' She sat.

He poured out two drinks and handed her a glass. 'Look, there's absolutely no need to get uptight about things.'

'Were you and Harwood . . .'

'Were we what?'

'Lovers?'

He was shocked.

'Is that why you won't admit to the police that you knew him; why you won't tell me the truth? Pierre, haven't thirty-one years of marriage taught you that I love you enough to ignore anything that happened before we were married? Of course I wouldn't welcome the idea; I don't think any woman would, however liberated she calls herself. But I'm not a Victorian flower and if men at sea can't get any other kind of sex . . .'

'For God's sake, do I look like a queer?'

'On the contrary.'

'Nothing would have induced me to have anything to do with him in that way. How the hell can you think such a bloody thing?'

'You keep lying to the police and to me.

Why do you sometimes hurt me so?'

'I've never willingly done that.'

'Haven't you? Don't you remember how I first learned you'd been awarded the OBE?'

He was bewildered by a question which reached so far back in time.

'Your mother told me after we'd become engaged. Not you, your mother. I never understood how you could be so careless of my feelings.'

'I don't know what you mean.'

'To let someone else tell me and deny me the extra pride of hearing it from you.'

'Pride? Don't you know what the letters OBE stand for?'

'Obviously not for what they really do.'

'Other bugger's effort. In the Merchant Navy, we weren't in the Forces so we couldn't be given fighting medals. When I lined up, waiting for the presentation, I got talking to the man next to me; he'd got his OBE for working twenty-five years in local government without being found out.'

'It doesn't matter what the hell he got his for. You got yours for outstanding bravery after the ship was torpedoed and nothing can alter that fact, not even if every other recipient was there for growing carrots. You saved those other men. How many other sixteen-and-a-half-year-olds would have done half as much?'

He shrugged his shoulders. 'Who knows

108

what anyone will do until he's put to the test?'

'That's not an answer . . . You won't answer anything. Why won't you tell the police you sailed with Harwood?'

'How many more times do I have to say it? I don't want to be reminded.'

'It's more than that. I know it is.' Quite suddenly, she began to cry.

The last time he'd seen her cry, years ago, had been when Rosalind had been very ill. He went over to the cocktail cabinet and began to speak as he poured himself a second and longer drink. 'I can still remember my feelings after the first torpedo hit us. Excited, instead of shit-scared. A sixteen-and-a-half-year-old idiot who thought it was all terribly adventurous. Until I saw a fireman who'd had most of his face steamed off . . .'

*   *   *

The Admiralty's Trade Division had routed the *Waitawea* home via Cape Horn. This was sufficiently unusual to cause the rumour mills to work overtime: the U-boat wolf packs had become masters of the Western Atlantic, the *Tirpitz* was loose in the Caribbean, the Panama Canal had been wrecked.

They rounded the Horn on a Sunday morning. For a romantic, nurtured on stories of windjammers under bare poles, in constant danger of being pooped, buying their lee rails

109

under green water (five men manned the braces, now only two remained), the morning would have been bitterly disappointing. The wind was a mere force five, the sea no more than choppy; true, the swell was heavy, but the ship scended easily and one could walk the main deck fore and aft without any fear of even being wetted by spray. And the island was only a dirty smudge on the horizon.

From the Horn, they steamed a course which kept them equidistant from the coasts of South America and Africa—reports made it clear that U-boats were active off both continents. Zigzagging was commenced, guns were constantly manned, and the look-out was stationed in the crow's nest, but the captain decided double watches need not be kept until they crossed the equator.

It was noon, on a Saturday. The sky was cloudless, the sun very hot, the sea pleasantly alive because of the swell; flying fish skimmed away from their bow wave, a distant whale blew.

Company's standing orders laid it down that noon sights should be taken by all officers except the chief officer and all cadets except for any day worker. On many ships, it was recognized that such a sextuplication of effort was wasteful—not to mentioned more conducive to possible dissension—and so only the second and one cadet took noon sights, but Captain Young believed that the company's standing orders had been engraved on tablets. He demanded that a full muster of officers and cadets shot the sun under his personal supervision, that the second, third, and fourth, carried out their calculations in the chartroom, that the cadets did the same in the wheelhouse, and that each man brought him a slip of paper on which was written the noon position, course and distance run from the previous noon position or alteration of course, average speed over the past twenty-four hours, average speed for the voyage, course and distance to the next alteration of course, and ETA. The slips of paper were examined closely to see if any of the answers differed markedly from average; if one did, its compiler was sent back to rework all his figures.

The cadets had naturally long since learned to collate their answers and then to check with one of the officers' work books—when the owner was out on the wing—before submitting their bits of paper since then there was less likelihood of placing the *Waitawea* in the middle of the Sahara. Tourkville was the last to hand in his piece of paper to the captain out on the wing. He waited for the reluctant grunt which would mean that his figures were accepted and he could carry on below, but this never came. There was a violent explosion that temporarily deafened and the ship shudderd and went on

111

shuddering with diminishing force for many seconds. Both he and the captain lost their balance and instinctively he reached out for support, by mistake grabbed the captain, and brought them both crashing to the deck.

He scrambled to his feet. But the captain lay as he had fallen and, seemingly indifferent to the fact that his ship had just been torpedoed, shouted that Tourkville had carried out a deliberate assault for which he would be logged.

(Considerably later, Tourkville was to look back on this extraordinary reaction to events and realize that in it lay the key to much of the captain's past behaviour. He had been suffering from what, for want of a more accurate description, could be called shell shock. In his middle fifties, he'd never overcome the mental trauma of having his previous ship bombed from under him, of being dragged down as she suddenly rolled over, and of nearly drowning. Instead of being given a fresh command as soon as possible, he should have been kept ashore for treatment.)

The second and third ran out on to the wing as the action-station bells started to ring. They stared down at the captain, for the moment not knowing what to do. The chief officer raced up the ladder from the boat-deck and he, in sharp contrast to his normal style, took immediate action. 'Get him on his feet.'

112

He swung round and stared aft. Because they were still steaming at full speed, the creamed area of water which marked the point at which they'd been hit was already astern. Between there and the ship trailed a growing line of flotsam, mainly shattered butter boxes. The deck at number four had been ripped jaggedly upwards, like an opened sardine can, and one of the hatch boards had, together with a strip of smouldering tarpaulin, been blasted up and over on to number five square. Water, flung up by the explosion, still streamed down from the deck-houses and deck.

The chief officer, shirtless because he had been resting on his bunk, asked the now upright captain what were his orders. The captain said the bloody boy was to be logged for assault and insubordination. The chief officer rapped out a series of commands; reduce to half speed (not slower, despite the possibility of wrenching open the hull still further, because they had to try to get out of range of the submarine), constant zigzag, second to go aft to assess the damage with the carpenter, carpenter to sound the after wells, third to work out course and distance to the nearest land and to write out this information for each boat, chief radio operator to transmit in clear their position.

As the interior engine-room indicator on the telegraphs swung round to half speed, to

113

the accompaniment of clanging bells, the mate went out to the end of the wing and stared down at the sea. Conditions could have been very much worse; they could have been a little better.

The captain crossed to where he stood and demanded to know if the boy had been logged. He ignored the question as he tried to gauge, on an almost complete lack of direct evidence, whether they dared to continue at half speed. The ship was answering the helm and moving easily, as if she had suffered only minor damage. Yet the torn and buckled deck was proof that the explosion had been anything but minor. Then he remembered that the cargo in number four lower hold, and middle 'tween, was butter, in half hundredweight boxes, and he realized that this densely packed, 'giving' wall of butter must have absorbed much of the force of the explosion. They would continue at half speed.

The second arrived back at the bridge, his face streaming with sweat. 'As far as I can tell, damage is confined to number four. There's a large hole in the hull which stretches below the waterline and some of the cargo's coming out, but not nearly as much as I'd expect. I reckon the explosion has welded the butter into a solid mass. Chippy says the tanks at four are making, but five are still dry . . .'

His words were cut short by a second

explosion and this flung them both to the deck.

The boiler room had been struck. Superheated steam belched out and roasted some men in seconds; others took a little longer to die. The sea flooded in, a cataract that overwhelmed and drowned. Both main dynamos had been sprung from their beds and all lights had failed. The third engineer, using a torch, switched over to emergency lighting. Firemen, greasers, and engineers, knowing that this time the ship was doomed, did not wait for the order, but began their desperate attempts to escape from hell. Some were courageous enough to try to save their mates as well as themselves, others knocked aside or trampled over the wounded to reach the ladders.

The ship was listing quickly. 'Boat stations,' ordered the chief officer.

In the wheelhouse, the loud-hailer system was still working and the third broadcast the order.

The list increased. Men reached the boat-deck and assembled by their boats. From the bridge, Tourkville saw two firemen, one supporting the other, stagger out of a doorway and he stared incredulously at the smaller one who appeared to have put on a mask. Then he realized, with a rush of nausea, that the 'mask' was composed of strips of flesh which had been flayed by

115

superheated steam.

There was a series of heavy rumbles from below and the ship shivered to each one. The list continued to increase. In the wheelhouse, a pair of binoculars slid off a for'd locker on to the deck, shattering one of the lenses; nautical tables and a cased sextant followed.

The chief officer, now having to hang on to the docking telegraph for support, said: 'Take command of your boats.' He looked at the captain, shrugged his shoulders.

Tourkville followed the third down the ladder to the boat-deck and then went along to number six boat, the captain's and the only one with an engine. This, as had all the others since leaving port, had been swung out and then lashed hard against fenders with quick release buckles; now only the buckles had to be released before the boat could be lowered.

The list suddenly increased sharply, sending men shuffling along the deck until they could regain their balance. Through the large ventilators by the funnel came the harsh sounds of destruction in the engine-room.

Still on the wing of the bridge, the chief officer stared down at the sea. Although the engines had been stopped by the force of the explosion, they were still making too much way for it to be safe to launch the boats. Yet how much longer did he dare leave the order to abandon ship?

'What is happening?' demanded the

captain, who'd not spoken for minutes.

'We're preparing to abandon ship, sir.'

'Have you logged the boy?'

'Yes.'

'For physical assault and insolence?'

'For both.'

He stepped out to pace the bridge, immediately lost his balance and fell hard against the dodger. 'Chief, we're going to have to abandon ship.'

'As soon as we've lost enough way, yes, sir.'

The ship was dying, perhaps too quickly.

In the cabins, drawers slid out, cupboard doors swung open, chairs crashed into bulkheads; in the pantries and mess rooms, glass, cutlery, plates and dishes, cascaded down; in the galley, soup, fried fish, roast pork, roast potatoes, peas, treacle tart, and custard, formed a nauseous mash on the deck; in the baker's shop, loaves tumbled into buns and cakes; in the butcher's shop, hunks of raw meat rolled or slid into an untidy pile against the inboard bulkhead.

The chief officer hauled his way up the sloping deck through the wheelhouse and out on to the port wing. Already, the list was too severe for the port boats to be launched. He cupped his hands around his mouth. 'Port crews to starboard boats.' The order had been expected and was carried out quickly, those too injured to move on their own being carried. Hanging on to support all the way, he returned to the starboard wing and once more studied the sea, balancing risk against risk, knowing that on his decision rested the lives of all those on the boat-deck. He spoke to the captain. 'We'd better abandon ship now, sir.'

'Very well.'

He waited to see whether the captain would finally resume command, but when the other didn't, gave the order. 'We'd better go to our boats, sir.'

The captain nodded. Clumsily, he followed the chief officer down the ladder, then he continued along the deck to his boat. He understood what was happening, but not that the men looked to him to order their actions. When he came to the for'd davit of number six, he stood and waited.

The bos'un, who'd come across from number five, of which he would have been in command, looked uncertainly at the captain. Finally, he could keep silent no longer. 'Hadn't we better start lowering away, sir?'

'Carry on.'

The bos'un detailed the second engineer and two seamen into the boat and ordered the coiled ladder, made fast to the deck, to be released. As the three men boarded, the ladder was pushed over the side; it uncoiled with an ever increasing speed and its end lashed the water.

In the boat, the engineer prepared to start the motor and the two seamen checked that the painter was fast and the lifelines, secured to the stay running between the davits, would run freely.

The bos'un in his gravelly, West Country voice, said: 'Timpson, Savage, stand by to lower; everyone else in the boat.'

It was Tourkville's duty to remain aboard until the boat had been lowered. He watched the men climb into the boat and pack themselves tightly on the thwarts.

'Stand by to lower.'

Timpson and Savage freed the quick release catches and the heavy canvas straps fell away. The boat began to swing, its rhythm slightly different from that of the ship's.

'Lower away.'

The boat was hoisted by an electrical motor and lowered under the force of gravity. Timpson, who was standing by the motor casing, lifted the control lever and the two wires began to slide through their single blocks, to the accompaniment of quick, snapping sounds. In the boat, seamen held boat-hooks ready in case the swinging became so heavy that they were in danger of crashing into the ship's side.

From the boat-deck, the sea had looked merely frisky; seen close to, it was filled with powerful movement. The AB standing by the after fall signalled to cease lowering; as they swung, he gauged the rhythm of the sea. He called for them to be lowered another six feet. They hung for a while as he waited for a rising sea. 'Let go.' They dropped until the rising sea caught and lifted them. Andrews, for'd, freed his hook; the after one refused to clear. 'Christ! I can't free it,' shouted the AB.

The sea began to retreat and they were in imminent danger of being upended as the bows dropped, but the stern remained fixed. In the split second available, Andrews slipped the for'd hook back on. The weight came on the falls and they briefly smoked from the strain; the boat shivered. The AB signalled for them to be raised three feet.

A noticeably larger sea swept in and the AB gave the order to lower. The moment the strain came off the falls, they released the hooks and this time both were successful. When the sea drew back, the boat was riding free, sheering out from the ship's hull because the painter was made fast to the for'd thwart and not to the bows.

On deck, the bos'un turned to the captain, but the latter still refused to command. The bos'un said: 'Timpson, Savage, down you go.'

Tradition had it that God's gift to seamen was the Pole Star; the Devil's, the Jacob's ladder.

At the best of times, a Jacob's ladder sorely

tested anyone who used it; at the worst of times—at sea, attached to a heavily listing ship now moving with very little sense of rhythm—it swung and jerked, and snubbed, with the violence and unpredictability of a bucking bronco.

Timpson, climbing down it sideways on, one leg to either side, reached the boat without too much trouble. Savage was half way down when a steeper, shorter sea rolled the ship heavily which sent the ladder swirling in towards the hull until tension snubbed it; Savage was plucked off by the force of the jerk. He screamed once before he hit the water. For some reason he was not wearing a lifejacket and he went deep and when he surfaced he was well astern of the lifeboat. He began to swim, not realizing what those above could clearly see, that he was being sucked into the hole in the hull. They watched him disappear.

The bos'un climbed nimbly down the ladder, making it all look easy. Then it was Tourkville's turn. The moment when Savage had been plucked off the ladder replayed in his mind. He saw the swimming man being sucked into his coffin . . .

He gripped the central rope of the ladder, swung his body round until he could reach over the side with his feet. Closing his mind to everything but the immediate present, he climbed down. After half a lifetime, hands

121

guided him into the boat.

Once aft, he stared up at the boat-deck, seemingly as high as any skyscraper. The upper half of the captain was visible. He was facing the bridge. A last farewell to a command which he had betrayed?

★   ★   ★

'I . . . I'm very silly,' Charlotte said, 'but I never realized how terrible it was.'

'Why should you? "The only full and honest teacher is experience." Tourkville refilled both their glasses. When he passed her hers, she took it with one hand, gripped his free hand tightly with her other. After a while, he gently freed himself and returned to his chair. He drank. He stared into the past.

'Do you mind going on?' she asked.

'We tried to get the engine going, but it wouldn't start. One of the engineers was supposed to have run it at regular intervals throughout the voyage, but obviously no one ever had because we discovered the fuel tank was full of sea water.'

'How on earth could that have happened?'

'It was put in to replace the petrol.'

'You're not trying to say that someone stole petrol from a lifeboat, putting survivors' lives at risk?'

'That's exactly right.'

'It's impossible. Nobody could possibly be

that vile.'

'The Liverpudlian stevedores found no difficulty. From other ships, they stole the emergency food from lifeboats.'

She shook her head, unable to comprehend such murderous behaviour.

'We rowed clear and waited with two other boats. The *Waitawea* had listed so quickly that I'd expected her to go down like a stone, but she didn't. She went slowly and I can remember thinking it was as if she was struggling to live . . . When she'd gone, there was just a circle of disturbed water, a few air bubbles breaking, and some flotsam, including a couple of the rafts. It's funny seeing your home turn into nothing more substantial than that.

'When she'd gone, the bos'un said to start rowing; nothing so useful in that sort of situation as being a bloody fool optimist. We were well away from the usual sea routes and according to the third's figures the nearest land was well over a thousand miles to the west. But row, boys, row.'

'What happened?'

'We fried, we cried, we died.'

'But thank God, some of you didn't.'

'Until we were rescued, that seemed to make us four the losers.'

'And Harwood was one of you?'

'Which taught me never to judge by appearances. Beforehand, I'd have said he'd have been one of the first to go. But then he did have Daisy kicking him back into life whenever he felt like dying.'

'But if what really happened was that you were together in the boat for twenty-four days . . .'

'Thirty-four,' he interrupted. 'Our Calvary went on a long time.'

'Thirty-four. Why keep on denying you knew him?'

'Because I want to bloody forget,' he said with sudden anger. He finished his drink and hurried out of the room.

CHAPTER TWELVE

Critics of the Far Eastern Pacific and Australasian Steamship Company, of whom over the years there had been many, were wont to claim that the last time the directors had had an original idea was back in nineteen-eleven when they'd decided to add an extra white bar in the top, staff side quarter of the house flag. In the past years, other shipping companies had modernized, rationalized, and specialized, and had built bigger and bigger ships after the experts had proved that size was the key to profitability, and as a result the traditional cargo and mailship had vanished and when there was a downturn in shipping the leviathans had cost so much to keep idle that the companies owning and running them had gone bankrupt. But the F. E. P. & A. (Food evil pay awful) had continued to build and run traditional style ships, none of more than twenty thousand tons, and the result of this backward thinking was that the company had made a loss in only two of the past twenty years.

The company owned the freehold of the head office, just off Leadenhall Street, which two years previously had come fifth in a list of the capital's ten ugliest buildings. The chairman was said to have been puzzled that anyone should worry about what a commercial office looked like. The entrance hall was large and gloomy, a suitable setting for the middle-aged lady at the reception desk. She listened to the DC and then immediately told him that no one in the building would be able to help him. He said he was sorry to hear that, but since this was an important police matter, perhaps he might have a word with someone just to confirm that she was correct. Grim-faced and vinegar-toned, she used the telephone to speak to the assistant marine superintendent; when she replaced the receiver she told him, in tones of some satisfaction, that he'd have to wait.

He wandered over to the stand in the

centre of the hall and studied the encased model of a cargo liner, built in nineteen-thirty-eight. He imagined himself on the boat-deck, a tropical moon shooting a shaft of silver across the water, a beautiful, passionate, nubile blonde by his side . . .

'Captain Ashcroft will see you now.' Reluctantly, the receptionist added directions on how to find the captain's office.

He reached the last office at the end of a gloomy corridor and knocked, entered.

Ashcroft was the epitome of the bluff sea captain who preferred life ashore. 'Sit down and tell me what's up. Nothing drastic, I hope? No one planting bombs aboard our ships?'

The DC sat. 'I've come to see if you can help in some inquiries we're making concerning a couple of blokes; one of 'em we know was on your ships, the other might have been.'

'What's the object of the exercise?'

'I can't really say, Captain. It's a request that's come through from another force and we don't know the details . . . The first name is Edward Pierre Darcy Tourkville, who was a cadet.'

'That's quite a name! And as a matter of fact, it seems to ring a bell, but for the moment I can't think why.'

'The other is John Harwood. He was a steward. We'd like to know if they ever sailed on the same ship at the same time.'

Ashcroft had been writing; now he looked up. 'I've got those. Now, which are the ships?'

The DC brought out his notebook, opened it, and flipped through the pages. 'Ready? *Waitawea*, *Wopotiki*, *Togotapao*, and *Maurangi*.'

'What?'

'Have I got the pronunciations all wrong?'

'That's not it. The *Waitawea* and the *Wopotiki* were lost during the war—every W ship went down. As far as I can remember, the *Togotapao* and the *Maurangi* survived the war, but they'll have ended up in breakers' yards years ago. D'you realize that none of these ships can have been afloat in the past thirty years?'

'No, I didn't. Like I said, we've no details . . . Is that going to make things difficult?'

'Bloody impossible, I'd say.'

'You don't keep records?'

'For a time. After that, they're out, or we'd all be stifled by the paperwork. Unless the two men are in the company pension scheme, I don't know there'll be any trace of them at all.'

'But perhaps you could just check?' The DC grinned. 'Then we can say everthing possible's been done and forget it.'

*   *   *

127

On Thursday, there was a message for the DC to ring Captain Ashcroft.

'Afternoon,' said Ashcroft, in his breezy manner. 'You're in luck. I've actually managed to find out something which may be of use.'

'That's great.'

'The crew lists have long since gone, but I had the idea of asking someone to check through the company's commonplace book—that's their name for the publicity scrapbook—and in it were several cuttings about the *Waitawea* and how only four survivors were rescued after thirty-four days in a boat. Tourkville, the only officer—if one allows such an exalted rank to a cadet—was awarded the OBE. That was why I seemed to know the name.'

'And there was a reference to Harwood?'

'He was one of the other survivors.'

'Then they did sail together.'

'To hell and back.'

'Yeah,' said the DC, who'd been born long after the war and was easily bored by the subject.

★ ★ ★

Detective-Inspector Jenkins ran the palm of his right hand over the top of his head, smoothing down his hair at the point where it was thinnest. 'I'm not up with what sort of relationship there was in those days between officers and crew and I'll accept that it could be possible a cadet wouldn't know the name of everyone aboard. But after thirty-four days in a lifeboat, there's no way Tourkville wouldn't have known who Harwood was. And after that experience, he's going to remember him to his dying day. So why's he denied over and over again that he's ever known Harwood?'

'The suggestion is that the memories are too painful to want to talk about them,' replied Burrow.

'Which could be true.'

'If one forgets the slip of paper found in Harwood's flat.'

'Which brings up the possibility of blackmail. I've been wondering about that. It provides the motive for the murder of Harwood . . . But that in turn raises a question—if Tourkville murdered him to cut short the blackmailing, who tried to murder Tourkville?'

'My reading of the situation is that no one did. There was a poacher who panicked or was warning Tourkville not to get too close. Don't forget, that's what he says; it's his wife who's so certain it was an attempt to murder him.'

'There is another possibility, isn't there? That he faked the whole scene. If it seems he was the subject of a murder attempt, we'll look on him as another victim, not a suspect. Then he deliberately makes light of the incident to us, but not to his wife, to add a left-handed corkscrew verisimilitude.'

'You're crediting him with a hell of a lot of guile.'

'Maybe too much for an essentially straightforward character? . . . Let's get back to the blackmail. What was the lever? And it's got to be a heavy one bcause there's the ten thousand in the safe, the flat which cost another fifty, and a high lifestyle. We could be looking at close on a hundred thousand.'

Burrow brought out his pipe and began to rub the bowl against his cheek. He spoke slowly, largely thinking as he went along. 'We can take it that they'd never met before the voyage. We've nothing to suggest they ever met after being rescued, that is until the possible blacking. So whatever the lever was, it looks like it comes from the time they were at sea together.'

'In one report from Etrington there was a note that Harwood was a queer.'

'You're suggesting Tourkville ran a course with him—would you say Tourkville was ever that way inclined?'

'Who the hell can judge from appearances alone? These days, announce that the next dance is the Gay Gordons and you get knocked down in the rush.'

'The wife might not know.'

'Could be. Tourkville's from the generation who didn't publish their little peculiarities. But would he cough up a hundred grand to hide the fact?'

'Maybe the wife holds most of the moneybags and she'd keep them tight shut if she learned the truth?'

'If that's so, where did he find the blackmail money? . . . In any case, the estate's his, not hers.'

'So where do we go from here?'

'You find out if, in fact, he was being blackmailed.'

'Ask him outright and we'll get a very dusty answer. Can we apply for an order to examine all his bank accounts?'

The DI shook his head. 'On the facts as we know them, an order would never be granted.'

'Then it's going to be difficult.'

'I'm sure you'll find a way,' replied the DI, bringing the conversation to an end.

★   ★   ★

Noyes entered the gunsmith at the north end of the high street. He passed a dummy in thornproof leggings and jacket, several game bags hanging from a multiple-hook stand, and a cardboard cut-out of a Mexican desperado around whose waist and chest were fastened several different types of cartridge belts. There was a long counter, under whose glass top were displayed Swiss army penknives, cartridge extractors, cleaning rods and squares, silver hip flasks and hand-warmers. Behind the counter, against the wall, was a glass-fronted gun cabinet in which were racked 12, 20, and .410 shotguns, .22 and .275 rifes, air rifles and CO_2 pistols. He waited for the assistant to finish talking to a customer who was wearing a country suit in a noisy check. Cockney masquerading as Cheltenham was his scornful judgement of the customer.

The assistant finally came along the counter and spoke to him. 'Can I help you?'

No 'sir', thought Noyes, although noisy-suit had been 'sir' again and again. Was it obvious that he wasn't intending to order a pair of Purdeys? 'CID. We're making certain inquiries and you may be able to help. What sort of sale is there for cartridges with size five shot?'

'I'd say it's quite considerable, although possibly six and seven are more popular.'

'Could you name who's bought size five in the past month?'

The assistant hesitated, then said primly: 'I think it would be best if you speak to the manager.'

The manager was tall and thin and he had an old-fashioned, grave, courteous style. He

132

waited until Noyes was seated in the comfortable armchair in front of the desk in the small office, then himself sat. Behind him, on the wall, hung a number of framed photographs from the shooting field. Like so many who had had a great deal to do with guns before it was discovered they should wear ear-mufflers, he was slightly deaf and frequently cupped a hand behind his right ear. 'Five shot is a normal size for something the size of a rabbit.'

'What about duck?'

'That's the size I recommend. As I expect you know, it's all a question of compromise. The larger pellet has greater striking power, but there are fewer of them in a cartridge so the pattern is not dense. If I remember rightly, in a one ounce charge the difference is some fifty pellets. To a good shot, that will be immaterial; to a poor one, it might well be the difference between killing and pricking.'

'Would you know who buys number five shot?'

'I doubt it, unless he's a regular customer.'

'What about Mr Tourkville?'

The manager's manner changed. 'He is one of our regular customers, yes, although now his custom is very much less than it used to be. I understand he conserves and so only shoots predators.'

'Does he buy number five shot?'

'I think I need to know the reason for the

question before answering it.'

'Inquiries.'

There was a brief and silent tussle of wills which the manager lost—after all, it was greatly in the interests of the shop to be on a friendly footing with the police. 'He normally buys five shot since his biggest worries are crows and magpies.'

★   ★   ★

The bus braked to a stop and Noyes jumped down on to the pavement. He walked along the road and turned into Grassington Crescent. It was growing dark and the forms of the houses were soon lost with distance so that they ceased to be a row of identical semi-detacheds, but could be allowed variety; here and there a light shone out. Peace and even a quiet beauty, he thought, with a rare flash of romanticism.

Carol was wearing an expertly cut, high-collared frock which emphasized the cool classicism of her longish face. He kissed her, hung up his mackintosh. 'What's for supper—I'm starving?'

'Hotpot.'

'Just what the doctor ordered. Plenty of black pudding, I hope?'

'Enough to invite Dracula.' She led the way into the kitchen. 'Pete, you've a few days' leave due, haven't you?'

'Ten, hoarded with all the fervour of a miser.'

'Take them off and we'll go somewhere.'

'Like the Seychelles?'

'If they're on offer.'

'Provided someone else is paying, sure. But what about your job?'

'I caught the old bitch in a good mood and she said that if I'm not away for more than a fortnight and it's before the middle of next month, OK.'

'Then if the Seychelles are full, I'll book us into a boarding-house in Blackpool.'

'You'll be there on your own, that's for sure . . . Couldn't we take the car over to France and have a bit of a tour?'

'A dirty weekend? When do we start?'

'Can't your mind ever rise above the one subject?'

'Are there others?' As he watched her lift a glass casserole dish out of the oven and put it on a board on the table, he thought that this light-hearted, perhaps to an outsider inane, banter epitomized the warm and frothy life together they'd first known: then, gradually so that it was only obvious in retrospect, things had changed. Why couldn't he learn to fight a little less?

She opened a drawer and brought out a ladle. 'There you are, help yourself and fish out as much of the black pudding as you can find. I'm not all that fond of it.'

'You don't know what's good for you.' He served himself generously, sat in the small dining alcove, and began to eat. 'It's good. If you need a recommendation as a cook, I'll give you one.'

'Just as a cook?' she asked, as she joined him at the table.

'Are you also good at something else?'

'Not back to that again? . . . Have you ever seen the Bayeux Tapestry?'

'I've never even heard of it.'

'Stop trying to make yourself out to be a cultural moron . . . It would be wonderful to go to Bayeux and see it. That's something I've always wanted to do.'

'It's the first time I've heard that.'

'Every wise woman keeps a few mysteries up her sleeve.'

'Sleeve?'

'For God's sake put a tourniquet around your mind and concentrate on eating.'

The telephone rang. He put his knife and fork down, but she said: 'I'll answer in case it's the station shouting for you.' She stood. 'I'm damned if you're working tonight, even if someone's assassinated the chief constable. I'll tell them you're out.'

She went through to the hall. Initially, he listened to her end of the conversation to discover whether it was the station, but as soon as it became clear that the caller was one of her friends, he lost interest.

A few minutes later she returned to the kitchen.

'If your grub's cold, change it for some still in the dish,' he suggested.

'It doesn't matter.'

It didn't immediately occur to him that her manner had changed completely. 'I reckon your idea of a trip in France is great. We can have a shufty at the tapestry and then a wander wherever looks good; maybe the châteaux district. Bert went over not so long ago and he said that it was lovely and if you keep away from the big hotels and restaurants it's no more expensive than over here and sometimes quite a bit cheaper. He had one of the best meals of his life in a small place near Alençon and it only cost eight quid a head. You try getting a meal round here for that, wine included.'

She made no comment.

He finally realized that her expression was now sharp, almost hard. 'Is something up, love?'

'Nothing that you'd find important.'

Her tone had been contemptuous. His reaction was immediate and automatic and he became aggressive. 'Who was that on the phone?'

'Lucy.'

'What was she after?'

'A bit of a chat.'

'Then it was a bitchy one.'

'In one way, I suppose it was; but not in the way you're meaning.'

'She's a right trouble-maker.'

'You reckon?'

'I know. You ask Tom Meecham if you don't believe me; he'll give you the lowdown on her. If I were you, I'd have as little as possible to do with her.'

'Really? Then think how much less informed our lives would be.'

'What's that supposed to mean? What's suddenly got into you? Before you talked to her, everything was fun.'

'Surely you can work things out?'

'She said something about me?'

'In passing.'

'That bitch never did anything in passing. What was she on about?'

'She mentioned that she saw you the other day.'

'Then I can reckon myself bloody lucky that I didn't see her.'

'Apparently you were far too busy for that to have happened.'

'Too busy doing what?'

'Chasing up a redhead who was so obvious that the small print could be read without glasses.'

He remembered the night when he'd gone to the pub to meet the informer who'd never turned up. 'That's what's put me into the deep-freeze? For God's sake, you don't think there was anything in me just talking to her?'

'No? How very disappointing for you. Don't say you're losing your touch. But of course it can happen when one gets older.'

'I went into the pub to meet a nark who didn't show. When I left, I ran into her.'

'From all accounts, that must have been quite a tactile thrill. Promising enough, anyway, to turn round and take her into the pub.'

'Where I bought her one drink.'

'Is that all it takes these days?'

'I bought her one drink and then came home.'

'Perhaps you should have been more generous and given her a second one.'

'Goddamnit, she asked me back to her place, but . . .'

'So one was enough after all. I'm not surprised.'

'I wasn't interested.'

'Now you're straining even my credulity.'

'Why the hell won't you believe me?'

'Perhaps because I've been married to you for five long years.'

Bitterly he remembered how earlier he had walked down the road and seen only peace and beauty. How stupid could a man get? Hadn't he yet learned that in any row of houses there would be at least one behind whose walls there was only bitterness and even hatred?

CHAPTER THIRTEEN

Charlotte was in the kitchen, peeling potatoes, when the front doorbell rang. 'I'll answer it.'

Ada, who was polishing a silver pheasant which had been presented to Tourkville's grandparents on their golden wedding anniversary, did not bother to speak.

Charlotte left and went along the passage into the hall and across to the heavy wooden front door. The caller was Noyes. 'Good morning, nice to see you again,' she said.

''Morning, Mrs Tourkville. Is your husband around?' he asked, not even trying to give the impression that he had started the day bright and cheerful.

'I'm afraid he isn't. He's gone off with Fred Doyle to a farm in West Sussex for the sale of a Sussex herd and I don't expect him back before the middle of the afternoon. And if the inquisition goes on for even longer than usual, he may be later than that.'

'Inquisition?'

'The get-together afterwards of disappointed buyers, during which battered egos are salved. I'm sure you can imagine the line. "I only bid for that cow for a bit of a joke and if someone's fool enough to offer a hundred more than it's worth, good luck to him."'' She smiled.

He briefly wondered why it was that one person had a smile that never left the starting grid whilst another had one that was a winner.

'I'm afraid you're having very bad luck in getting hold of him, but from his point of view at least it means he can keep up a pretence that he's busy . . . But come along in and tell me if I can help. Perhaps you've a message you'd like passed on?'

They went into the green room.

'Would you like a coffee? Or perhaps something stronger, always assuming the sun's over the yardarm. And why shouldn't we do that, since in any case we have to assume the yardarm?'

His ill-temper was no match for her warm friendliness. 'Thanks, Mrs Tourkville, but I'm fine as I am.'

Ada came in, carrying the silver pheasant. She crossed to the nearest display cabinet and carefully put the pheasant down on a square of felt. That done, she looked at Noyes, then left. Wondering whether I'd try to pinch it, he thought. The idea amused him; minutes before it would have angered him.

'Now, how can I help?' asked Charlotte.

'I came to ask your husband a question or two about shooting.'

'I used to load for him when he shot regularly, so I might know at least some of the answers. try me.'

'Would shot size five be common?'

'In the ordinary shooting field, nearly as common as six, I'd say.'

'Your husband doesn't shoot regularly any longer, but he still shoots?'

'He's keen on conservation these days, especially duck, so that means making certain the predators never become too numerous.'

'Would he have any size five cartridges?'

'I've no idea.'

'Can you check for me?'

'Yes, of course.'

'And if he does, would you let me have one?'

He watched her leave. She had the figure and the easy, graceful movements of a woman twenty years younger. He wondered if her kids had ever stopped to think how lucky they were to have a mother who had the time, financial backing, and warmth, to give them a perfect upbringing? Probably not. Kids were so often selfish little bastards. He'd certainly been; literally. A bastard who'd sometimes thought about his mother with resentment because she hadn't a husband, instead of with gratitude for all she'd done to keep the home going . . .

Charlotte returned and handed him a cartridge.

'Thanks,' he said, as he slipped it into his coat pocket.

'How's that going to help?'

'Frankly, I'm not certain that it is. But the more that we can compare, the more likely we are to find an answer,' he said with deliberate vagueness.

'Have you any idea who tried to kill my husband?'

'Not yet, I'm afraid . . . Which does bring up the question again of whether there's anyone who might hold a grudge against him—he had to sack a farmworker not so long ago, I think?'

'Thompson. Fred Doyle caught him stealing some of the farm stuff. But Thompson would never do such a terrible thing; he's a weak little man.'

'Things are never that straightforward. It doesn't take much strength to pull a trigger.'

'Maybe not physically, but it must take mental strength of a kind and I just don't think he's got that.'

'Do you know where he went after leaving here?'

'As a matter of fact, I do. When we had the unpleasant task of telling him to leave his tied cottage, I said we ought to offer him some money to help; my husband said that was absurd since we were sacking him. But he has a wife and four kids and I couldn't help thinking about how difficult things would be for the wife until he found another job; it's so often the wife who suffers. Anyway, we gave

143

them some money, but only after they'd found a place so we could be certain they would be leaving; and I made sure she had it and not he. Someone he knew had been left a place in Marsham Avenue, on the other side of Watlingham, and he's there until he can find another job.'

'You wouldn't know the number, I suppose?'

'I'm afraid not.'

'No matter. If we need to find him, it won't be difficult.'

'I'm sure he couldn't have been the person who was trying to kill my husband.'

'Maybe not.'

'You don't mean that, do you? You don't believe one can truly judge what kind of character a person has?'

'To be honest, no, I don't.'

'Then you're like my husband.'

'It's safest to think that way these days.'

'What a cynical thing to say! Shall I tell you what kind of a person you are? You're not nearly as cynical as you try to make out. Now, am I right or wrong?'

'The accused is allowed to remain silent if to speak might incriminate himself.'

She laughed.

'I'd better be moving on, Mrs Tourkville.'

Her expression changed. 'I hope to God you find who it was.'

'We'll do our best.'

She forced herself to relax and, once he was standing, said: 'I've enjoyed talking to you. I hope you'll be back.'

He hoped he wouldn't. She had said that it was so often the wives who suffered. She could be in danger of learning how brutally correct that was.

*   *   *

Tourkville drove into the courtyard and parked the green Volvo in what had been the coach-house. Once in the hall, he called out Charlotte's name.

'Just coming,' she shouted from upstairs. Seconds later, she appeared. 'I was searching for a knitting pattern. Well, what sort of a day did you have?'

'A complete waste of time. The animals all had bad conformations and there were a couple of idiots who kept pushing up the prices to absurd levels.'

She laughed as she started down the stairs.

'And what's so humorous about my having had a thoroughly frustrating day?'

'I'm a witch.'

'That's interesting, but it explains nothing.'

'I can foretell the future without looking at the stars or into a crystal ball.'

'You're confusing witches with astrologers and clairvoyants. If I hadn't been married to

145

you for a long time, I'd say you were tight.'

'Which means you cannot conceive of my going on a binge? No mystery left in our ancient marriage? How very sad.'

'Cut the cackle and tell me what it's all about.'

'One of the detectives was here this morning.' She reached the foot of the stairs. 'He wanted a word with you, but I told him you wouldn't be back until after the inquisition. I had to explain what I meant and I said that if you failed to buy any animals you'd gather with all the other frustrated farmers and you'd swap judgements on how poor the animals were, how you'd only bid for a joke, and how stupid were the people who'd bought them.'

'Which makes me not only a blimp, but a wholly predictable blimp?'

They went into the green room, where he poured out a whisky for her and a gin and tonic for himself. 'Which detective was it?'

'The young one, Noyes. If you get to know him, he's really quite pleasant.'

'Provided you like porcupines.'

'It's a case of jollying him along and not reacting to his brash manner.'

'You jolly him along and not react, I'll stick to my first opinion of him. What did he want this time?'

'To know a little about shooting—was number five shot used a lot and did you use

146

it? And could he have one of your cartridges.'

'You gave him one?'

'Yes, I did. There was no reason why not, was there?'

'None that I can think of. But why did he want it?'

'I didn't really understand. I don't know if that's because he was a bit vague or I was being stupid . . . Oh, and one other thing. He'd heard about Thompson and wanted his present address. He seemed to think it might have been Thompson who shot at you.'

'Then he now thinks it was deliberate?'

'He didn't really say one way or the other. But if he doesn't think it's still a possibility, why should he be bothering about Thompson?'

Tourkville shrugged his shoulders.

*　　*　　*

Noyes passed the cartridge across the desk to Burrow.

Burrow held it between forefinger and thumb. 'What are you going to do with it?'

'Send it off to see if the lab can make a useful comparison with the shot I dug out of the tree.'

'You reckon they might?'

'I'd say there's a chance.'

'Then you're going along with the DI that Tourkville could have been setting up a red herring.'

'That's right.'

'But the wife says he was in the house when the shots were fired.'

'Have you never known a wife to help her husband?'

'She's a liar?'

'Not in the usual sense. Just ready to stand by her husband, whatever.'

'"The path of duty sometimes lies in more than one direction . . ." By the way, there's a bit more news from Etrington. When they carried out a second search of the flat, they turned up a couple of balls of dried-up earth which had obviously come off a shoe or shoes, yet all Harwood's were as clean as a whistle and even the insteps were polished. So he wouldn't have walked anywhere muddy unless he had to, which means there's a chance the two balls dropped off the murderer's shoes. It could be an idea to take samples from the land around Highland Place and send them off for comparison.'

*   *   *

The tests on the shot and the earth were held in different laboratories, but coincidentally the results both came through on the Thursday.

Burrow massaged the bowl of his pipe. 'Hardly conclusive.'

'But indicative,' argued Noyes.

'Only if you've decided beforehand where you're heading.'

'Haven't we?'

'I wish I'd half your self-confidence . . . Damnit, I don't see Tourkville as a murderer.'

'I read that everyone's a murderer, provided there's a strong motive and opportunity.'

'You believe that sort of crap?'

'If we're on the right track, Tourkville killed because he was being blackmailed. He'd paid out close on a hundred thousand. That sort of money must have drained even his resources. Suppose that to pay out any more would threaten the estate—wouldn't he kill to prevent such a catastrophe?'

'I suppose it's just possible,' replied the detective-sergeant doubtfully. He put his pipe down on the desk. 'All right, let's assume for the moment that that's how it was. Then what was he being blackmailed over? What was so dangerous to him that first he paid out a hundred grand, then he murdered?'

'It has to do with his time at sea.'

'That's not much of an answer.'

'It would become a whole lot stronger if we asked for a court order to check through his bank accounts.'

'And you reckon we'd ever get it on this sort of evidence?' Burrow tapped the papers in front of himself.

'The two lots of shot are similar in comparison. Both lots of soil contain Torticelian clay and animal dung.'

'Can you imagine what defence counsel would do with that sort of evidence? He'd have a field day. Similar in composition? Wouldn't all cartridges made by the same company at any one time have shot of the same composition? How many tens of thousand of cartridges does that encompass? What was the exact retail distribution of those tens of thousands of cartridges? Can the sale of each and every one of them be traced out? . . . And the earth. Torticelian clay? Surely that's fairly common, especially in the South-East? And isn't dung found wherever there are animals? . . . I could go on for hours.' He began to pack his pipe with tobacco.

'All right, as defence counsel you'd have yourself a field day. But we don't need to prepare the evidence against meeting him, all we've got to do is convince a local magistrate we're talking sense. And if we chose to go before one of the dozy ones—and people don't come much dozier than a couple of 'em—we shouldn't have any difficulty. Similar shot, similar earth, and forget the questions. Add that evidence to the rest we've got and we're home and dry.

'What rest? We've nothing worth a damn.'

150

'Suppose it's proved that Harwood had been to Highland Place recently? How would things look then?'

'You've proof he had?'

'Not yet. But if he was blacking Tourkville, it's a thousand to one he must have been; apart from anything else, he'd want to know how high to pitch the black.'

Burrow lit his pipe.

CHAPTER FOURTEEN

Noyes, wearing wellingtons, walked round the end of the Dutch barn and became aware of a pungent odour. He went across to where Weight was servicing a tractor. 'God, what a stink!'

Weight carefully screwed on the cap of a can of hydraulic fluid. 'How d'you mean?' he asked, his soft voice heavily laced with a Kentish accent.

'Something round here stinks like a dozen dead cats.'

Weight sniffed the air. 'I can't smell nothing but the silage and there's nowt wrong with that.'

'If it's silage I'm smelling, there's everything wrong with it.' Noyes looked across at a pen in which several bullocks were temporarily being held and thought that he'd

151

have to be paid rich money to work with animals that ate anything as stinking as silage.

Weight carried the can into the nearby shed. Noyes followed him and stared round at the forklifts, ditching arm, circular hedge cutter, hole digger, tedder, balers, silage cutter, flail mower, tipping trailers, silage trailer, second tractor, and ancient combine harvester. 'You've a fair bit of equipment.'

'You don't do much farming without . . . You can give us a hand to move that old cutter.'

The grass cutter was generously covered with thick black grease. As soon as it was fast in its new position, Noyes asked for a rag.

Weight grinned. 'Not used to getting your hands dirty?' He found a rag and handed it across.

Noyes carefully cleaned his hands. 'I've come to see if you can recognize someone.'

'Who?'

'I'll show you.' He put the rag down, brought an envelope out of his pocket and from this extracted a photograph which he handed across.

Weight studied it. 'He don't look very healthy.'

It had been impossible to judge from his lugubrious expression whether the remark had been meant seriously or had been a piece of macabre humour. 'That's not surprising, seeing he's dead,' Noyes said irritatedly.

152

'Never clapped eyes on him.'

Noyes took the photograph back and replaced it in the envelope. 'His real name was Harwood, but recently he'd been calling himself Harris. Ever heard anyone talk about John Harris who came from Etrington?'

'Can't say as I have. Did he have something to do with the shooting and Mr Tourkville?'

'Not directly, because he was dead by then . . . Heard anything more about that?'

'I ain't. Why should I?'

'You might have been down at the pub and listened to people talking.'

'Don't go to the pub more'n I have to.'

Did one ever actually have to? wondered Noyes.

Twenty minutes later he was speaking to Doyle, in the corner of a large field in which a number of cows were running with a bull.

'It was a gippo,' Doyle said, shielding his eyes against the sun as one of the cows caught his attention.

'Why d'you say that?'

'Because there ain't no one else would shoot so wild or stupid.'

Noyes handed him the photograph of Harwood. 'Have you ever seen this man around the place?'

Doyle looked at the photograph for a long time, then shook his head. He returned his attention to the cow which was quite definitely tending to keep apart from the rest of the herd, an action which always worried him when the cow in question was not about to calve.

✱   ✱   ✱

Charlotte heard the car drive into the yard, went out, and met Tourkville as he walked out of the garage. 'How did it go?' she asked anxiously.

'Between us, we persuaded Salting that our figures accurately show a projected profit so he finally agreed to advise head office to hold off; at least for the moment, we can forget having to sell up any of the land.'

'Thank God for that! . . . I just can't imagine how head office could have been so stupid as to put a small-minded man in charge of a country branch.'

'Not small-minded, just very careful. And from their point of view, that's great. It's impossible to think of him fiddling the books, playing the foreign exchange markets, or doing any of the other interesting things that bank employees sometimes get up to if they're adventurous types.'

They entered the house and went through to the kitchen. 'Something smells good,' he said.

'Belly of pork cooking in cherry brandy.'

'The thought makes me twice as hungry as I was . . . I'll just go and put these papers in the office.'

'Pierre . . .' She stopped.

'Yes?'

'There's something I haven't really understood. I know farm land has dropped in value so that our overall capital security isn't what it was, but it's still far more than the overdraft and what Dower Farm cost. If we've been repaying reasonably, why's the wimpy man fussing so?'

'It's not that simple.'

'What isn't? After all, it's not long ago that you said things weren't going too badly for us, however the rest of farming was doing. And you've not recently had to buy any machinery. So surely you have been repaying in full?'

'No,' he answered with obvious reluctance. 'I told you that the other day.'

'Then where's the money gone?'

'These days, it just goes.'

'But . . .'

'Cut out this third degree. You cope with your problems, I'll cope with mine.' He left.

She was more worried than ever. He had a temper—she'd have respected him less if he hadn't—but he had never before shown it in a matter such as this. They'd always worked as a financial team, each conversant with all the facts and equally concerned with the decisions. Yet now he was refusing to discuss a question which bothered her. Where had that money gone? One possible answer immediately came to mind. A woman. She was furious with herself for being so disloyal as even to consider such a possibility.

Three-quarters of an hour later, his normal good humour was fully restored. As he carved the pork on the sideboard in the dining-room, he told her that he'd met the Frewins in Watlingham and Diana wanted her to ring and fix a date for dinner. He carried the plates over to the table, handed her one, sat. She helped herself to mashed potatoes and beans, passed the dishes across. 'I saw Fred earlier on and he said the detective had been around, asking him and George questions.'

'In connection with the shooting?'

'I suppose so, though apparently not directly. He showed them a photograph of the man who died up in Etrington and asked if they'd ever seen him.'

'Why do that?'

She was disturbed by his sudden tension. 'I can't really make that out. Harwood died days before the shooting here.'

'What did they tell him?'

'That they'd never seen him, of course. Why should they have said anything else?'

'No reason.'

Yet there clearly was a reason. She shivered. She didn't know what threatened and frightened him, only that something did.

Since the house would not be in Thompson's name, Noyes did not waste time checking through directories, but drove straight to Marsham Avenue. He stopped at the first bungalow and asked the woman who opened the front door if she knew Thompson. She said she didn't, but she was fairly new to the district. He'd reached the front gate when she called out that she'd just remembered a couple with a load of noisy children had moved into No. 41 not so long ago—could they be the people he was looking for?

No. 41, also, a bungalow, showed obvious signs of neglect—peeling paint, overgrown privet hedge, weeds in the crazy-paving. In the tiny porch were a broken fire-engine and a rag doll, more rag than doll. From inside there came the sounds of children bawling. And it was called domestic bliss, he thought, as he pressed the doorbell.

A man of his own age and build, unshaven, his shirt collarless, opened the door. 'Mr Thompson?'

'That's me.'

'Detective-Constable Noyes, CID.'

Thompson could not conceal his uneasiness.

'I'm wondering if you can identify a photograph.'

As his confidence returned, Thompson's

157

manner became slightly cocky. 'Who would this be, then?'

'It might be best if I came in?'

'Oh! Sure.'

The narrow hall was littered with discarded toys. A boy came out of the kitchen and, sucking his thumb, stared at Noyes. Back in the kitchen, a younger child began to wail.

'Who is it?' a woman shouted.

'Someone as wants a word with me.'

'Then Billy, you come on back in here.'

The boy, still sucking his thumb, returned into the kitchen. Perhaps it was only coincidence, but the wailing increased and a third child began to shout.

'It's a bit noisy,' said Thompson.

'Just a bit.' Carol wanted to start a family before she was much older. Would she remain of the same mind if she came here?

'Let's go in there.'

The front room was as untidy as the hall; a newspaper was strewn across a chair, several colouring books were on the floor, three empty beer cans stood on the mantelpiece, and against the far wall was a plastic pot which, Noyes was thankful to note, was unused.

He sat in an armchair that was beginning to disintegrate. 'The last place you worked at was Highland Place, but you weren't there for very long?'

'I didn't get on with them, that's what.'

158

'Who didn't you get on with—Fred Doyle?'

'Thick old bastard.'

'How d'you make out with the Tourkvilles?'

'Them? They've always got a bad smell under their noses. And when she went on about helping my missus and the family, I nearly told her . . . It's easy enough to be big and generous when you're rich.'

'Easy, but not frequent; most times the rich won't give you the change from a five P. piece. Sounds like you resent Mrs Tourkville helping your family?'

'All I was saying was . . .' He stopped.

'Sometimes, it's better not to say.'

Thompson was mystified by the detective's sudden antagonism.

Noyes produced the photograph of Harwood and passed it across. 'Have you ever come across him?'

Thompson studied the photograph for several seconds. 'I reckon I've seen him around.'

'Around where?'

'When I was on the Highland farm.'

'You're certain?'

'Well, in this photo he ain't exactly the same, but . . . Yeah, it's him, all right.'

'How did you meet him?'

'I was up by the road in the five-acre, doing some tedding, and he wanted to know how to get to the house.'

The net was closing, Noyes thought; yet any satisfaction he might have gained was countered by the unwelcome knowledge that Charlotte Tourkville must also be caught up by that same net.

CHAPTER FIFTEEN

Jenkins's friendly manner, and his carefully cultivated habit of frequently appearing naïvely surprised by something a sharp, intelligent man would have known or guessed, made many of those he questioned think, until it was too late, that he was rather dim.

Tourkville initially imagined that his story was being accepted without any reservations. 'No, as I think I said just now, I didn't meet Harwood again after we'd been picked up and landed. I meant to keep in touch with all three of them, of course; when you all go through an experience like that, you do. But the truth is, a unique experience shared doesn't mean one's anything else in common. Even if that isn't a popular sort of thing to say today.'

'But true,' agreed Jenkins. 'It's like someone once said, you can't make a friend, you can only meet him.'

Very philosophical, thought Noyes sardonically.

'Harwood wasn't present when you were awarded the OBE?'

'No, he wasn't because he didn't get anything. I only did because nominally I was in command of the boat after the old man died.'

'Why d'you say "nominally"?'

'Because after the bos'un died fairly early on, and with the captain in a different world, I was the only one who wore a peaked cap; didn't matter that I was only sixteeen and a half, on my first voyage, and didn't know a damn thing about surviving in an open boat in the tropics.'

Charlotte spoke sharply, annoyed by the way in which he was belittling himself. 'You saved the lives of the others.'

'I didn't, an ordinary seaman called Andrews did. He made us fight on when all we wanted to do was die. He made me give the orders because I had the rank, but he had to tell me what those orders were . . . It's funny how authority goes with rank, irrespective of the man who holds it; logically, we'd only respect the rank and allow it authority if we could respect the man. But I suppose there'd be very little discipline in the forces if most people started thinking like that. Wouldn't be much good for politicians' self-esteem, either . . . But you didn't come here to hear my opinions of authority and politicans . . . No, I didn't meet Harwood again, or hear anything about him until I was told that it was he who had died in Etrington, under a different name.'

'So you wouldn't have any idea why he'd changed his name?'

'None at all.'

'I suppose you are quite certain that you never did meet him again?'

'Of course.'

'There's no chance you might have forgotten such a meeting?'

'Rather unlikely, in the circumstances.'

'True enough . . . But, you know, you did assure us for quite a while that you didn't know anyone called Harwood; then it turned out you'd sailed with him and he'd been one of the survivors.'

'I've explained that. The memories hurt too much to want to recall them.'

'Quite. But that does have me wondering if you're denying meeting Harwood again for the same reason?'

'I've said over and over again . . .'

'The fact is, isn't it, that you met him about a year ago?'

'No,' said Tourkville harshly.

'He was in the neighbourhood.'

'If he was, I didn't see him.'

'That's odd, because he was asking how to get to this house.' Jenkins turned to

Charlotte. 'Perhaps, Mrs Tourkville, you had a word with him?'

'No.'

'Of course, you might have done so without knowing who he was.'

'If he'd wanted to speak to my husband, I'd have asked him his name.'

'Perhaps he gave another false name. Would you mind looking at a photograph of him and telling me if you do remember meeting him? I'm afraid it was taken after death, but I don't think you'll find it at all horrifying.'

'My wife did not meet him,' said Tourkville.

'I'm sure you won't mind us just confirming that. In our work, confirmation of the negative is often just as important as of the positive.'

'If she . . .'

'Let me see the photograph,' cut in Charlotte. Jenkins stood and handed it to her. 'No, I have never seen him,' she said.

Jenkins took the photograph back and returned to his chair. 'Then we must presume, I suppose, that he came so far and no farther.'

'If the man you're talking about was he,' said Tourkville.

'It was a fairly definite identification . . . Assuming it was him, can you suggest why he should turn up after all these years?'

'It's not a presumption I'm prepared to make.'

'I see.' Jenkins showed no sense of irritation. 'Then we've just about covered everything.' He stood. 'Thanks for your help.' He sounded as if he meant that.

Charlotte said: 'Why do you go on and on asking my husband questions?'

Jenkins looked perplexed. 'Mrs Tourkville, there has been a case of murder.'

'Are you suggesting he knows anything at all about that?'

'I hope I've not suggested anything other than that we're trying to discover as much as we can about the dead man's history . . . Which reminds me that in spite of my brave words, there is one more question I have to ask your husband. Mr Tourkville, just for the records, where were you on the night of Tuesday, the sixteenth of last month?'

'What's it matter?'

'Simply a case of dotting the i's and crossing the t's.'

'I was here. I didn't spend a night away all month.'

'Thank you. Then now we really can go and leave you in peace.'

At the front door, Jenkins shook hands with friendly courtesy; Noyes merely nodded.

Tourkville closed the door and turned. Charlotte had come into the hall. 'Why did you lie?' she asked.

'What on earth are you getting at? Look, I must go out and . . .'

'You know you weren't here every night last month. You spent a couple of days in Oxford because of the annual general meeting of the club.'

'Did I? . . . Yes, of course. I'd forgotten.'

'Are you sure?'

'That's a funny sort of a question. If I'd remembered, I'd have told them.'

'Would you?'

'For God's sake, isn't it enough to have them wasting my time asking bloody silly questions, without having you join in?'

'Are you going to ring now and tell them you've made a mistake?'

'No.'

'Why not?'

'Because it's irrelevant.'

'But the sixteenth is one of the days you were away.'

'It's still irrelevant.'

'Harwood did come here, about a year ago, didn't he?'

'No,' he replied harshly.

'Pierre, I saw you talking to him. And when I asked you who he was, you told me he was looking for casual work, but at his age you certainly weren't going to give him any.'

'You're mixing him up.'

'I'm not . . . Something terrible's going on.'

165

'That's being ridiculous.'

'I wish to God it were. Originally, you lied about ever having known Harwood. Just now you lied about meeting him. Why? Why? Why? Please tell me. I want to help . . .'

'Every time they ask questions, it brings back memories. Can't you understand they make life a nightmare?'

'Why?'

'What d'you mean, why?'

'You may only have been sixteen and a half, but you had the courage of twice that; you went into hell, but you fought your way out of it because you always will if there's even the slightest chance. Remembering would be terrible, but for you there'd also be pride. So there has to be something more, something much worse. Pierre, I don't care how awful the truth is . . .' She stopped as he went outside, slamming the front door shut behind himself.

Slowly, feeling the ice inside her, she went through to the kitchen.

★   ★   ★

Jenkins drove with an élan that was strange, considering that in almost every other respect he was of a deliberate character. 'Well, what do you say that all adds up to?' he asked, as he took a corner at speed. 'Did you notice her expression when he said he hadn't been away the previous month?'

'Yeah,' replied Noyes briefly, as he pressed down an imaginary brake as they approached another and sharper corner.

'He was away. Just as he met Harwood. When a husband intends to lie, he ought to keep his wife out of the room.'

'Maybe she wouldn't have that.'

'Are you saying she knows all the answers?'

'I'd take a hefty bet she doesn't. But she knows enough to be worried sick.'

'And from the look of things, with cause . . . We'd better do two things. Turn up proof that he was away from the house on the sixteenth, and try to locate the two other survivors, if still alive, and discover if they can suggest what gave Harwood the handle to black Tourkville.'

*   *   *

The DC spoke to the formidable lady behind the reception desk at the offices of the Far Eastern Pacific and Australasian Steamship Company and asked to speak to Captain Ashcroft.

She studied him. 'You've been here before.'

'That's right.'

'Just under a fortnight ago.'

'You've a first-class memory.'

She was impervious to flattery. 'You can't

167

see Captain Ashcroft.'

'I won't keep him for long.'

'You can't see him because he's up in Hull.'

'Then perhaps I could have a word with someone who can have a shufty through the company's commonplace book for me?'

Five minutes later, he was talking to Lyons, a precise, desiccated, middle-aged man who thought of ships mainly as figures in accounts. 'You did say forty-five years ago?' Lyons asked in his dusty voice.

'That's right.'

'It's a very long time ago.'

'Even before I was a twinkle in my dad's eye.'

Lyons did not approve of such doubtful flippancy. Tight-lipped, he left the room. Several minutes later he returned with a large leather- and canvas-bound ledger. 'Do you know the exact date that the *Waitawea* was sunk?'

'The twenty-seventh of November.'

He turned pages, then read, running his forefinger down a page. 'There are three newspaper cuttings, plus a cross-reference to a fourth.'

'Do any of them give the addresses of the survivors?'

'Only in very general terms . . . Cadet Tourkville came from East Kent, Harwood from Cardiff, Smith from Portsmouth, and

168

Andrews from Stepney.'

'What about the fourth reference?'

'That is in another volume.'

'D'you think you could check it out?'

Lyons carried the book out, returned with another, similar one. He briefly searched in this, then said: 'It's a reference to a V-2 incident in which a public house received a direct hit and nine people were killed and twenty-seven injured. Andrews, one of those killed, is named because of the fact that he'd been a survivor of the *Waitawea*.'

CHAPTER SIXTEEN

'Just for a moment,' Carol said, 'you looked like you'd discovered you'd forgotten to send off the winning pools coupon.'

'You'll know when that's happened because I'll cut my throat,' replied Noyes.

'Do it somewhere where it's not too difficult to clear up the mess, will you?'

'That's all that matters?'

She laughed.

She had the kind of laugh that made a man think he could jump over the moon.

'I'd better rush, love, or the old bitch will give me another lecture for being late . . . D'you want me to take the bus for a change?'

'That's all right, use the car—it looks as if

it's going to bucket down at any minute and if you have to walk at the other end, you'll be drenched.'

'But I've had the car every day for ages.'

'My second name's self-sacrifice.'

She came forward and kissed him lightly. 'There's your reward.'

'Is that all?'

'Is your third name greedy? . . . There's a good film on in town; the new Spielberg. Is there any chance you could get off smartly tonight and we could see it?'

'I'll be back by six so we can grub out first.'

'You mean that?'

'Cross my heart four times.'

'Why the repetition? Do you have to convince yourself as well as me?' She kissed him again, then hurried out of the kitchen.

He followed her into the hall. 'We're parked in front of the Apses,' he said as she picked up an umbrella.

'Then I hope she doesn't see me or she'll moan like hell.' She opened the door and went out.

'Tell her someone was parked in front of our place.'

'She'll just say we were stupid to let 'em.'

He watched her walk out on to the pavement and turn to her left. He shut the front door. Ten minutes before he need move; time for another cup of instant.

As he added water to the little already in

the kettle, he thought that their emotional relationship resembled a roller-coaster ride; one minute climbing up into the skies, the next hurtling down into the depths. After she'd learned about his meeting with Judy, she'd become an ice maiden with a razor-sharp tongue. This had provoked him to say and do anything that would wound; it was yet another battle he must not lose. Then one night he'd come home worn out and bitterly frustrated—a long stake-out had been inadvertently rendered nugatory at the last moment. His supper had been laid out in the kitchen, together with a curt note that she'd gone to bed. When he'd entered the bedroom, she'd carefully not bothered for some time to look up from the book she'd been reading, but when she finally had, her concern had been immediate. 'Has something terrible happened?' she'd asked. He'd shaken his head. 'I'm just so bloody tired I'm dead on my feet.' 'You fool, why d'you let them drain you dry? Come here.'

Someone had once said that reconciliation was love's aphrodisiac.

He returned to the present, made the coffee, drank it, left the house and walked down to the bus stop. It seemed the fates were determined to keep his day a sunny one since a bus turned up in under a minute.

At the station he went up to the CID general room and began to check through his work to decide on priorities, but was interrupted by the internal telephone; Burrow wanted a word with him.

'About your last meeting with Tourkville. I gather he denies ever having met Harwood, but according to the old man it's obvious he did, as Thompson claimed. So maybe Doyle saw Harwood, never mind what he said. Question him again and if he remains uncooperative, pressure him.'

'Pressure him? He's out of the feudal age. God sits on the right hand of Edward Pierre Darcy Tourkville. If he'd seen Tourkville throttling Harwood, he'd deny everything out of a sense of dumb loyalty.'

'You're nuts,' said Burrow good-humouredly. 'And another thing. Get hold of Mrs Tourkville and question her . . .'

'Why drag her back into this?'

'What's that?' Surprise raised Burrow's tone. 'Did you have a heavy night?'

'Yeah. The fourth bottle of gin really creased me.'

'You must be getting soft . . . When you've got her talking, find out where her husband really was on the sixteenth/seventeenth.'

'And how in the hell am I supposed to go about doing all that?'

'Don't bother me with the problem—I've a DC who's going to work his butt off until he finds the answer.'

172

As Noyes walked away from Doyle's cottage, he sourly reflected that he couldn't have been more correct. Doyle had seen nothing and heard nothing; not even a session of *peine forte et dure* would alter that.

He drove along the road which was bordered by a coppice until he reached the gates of Highland Place. He turned into the drive. At the beginning of the case, he would have found it impossible to accept that Tourkville could have murdered in order to preserve the estate, as opposed to his financial interest in the estate, but now he could. Yet . . .

Charlotte spoke angrily. 'My husband is away for the morning. Do you really have to keep on bothering him like this? He is a very busy man.'

'I'm sorry, but our inquiries . . .'

'I fail to understand why you still believe that he can in any way be connected with what's happened.'

For the first time, she was speaking with the supercilious disdain of the rich when faced by something they disliked. But, he told himself, it was worry which caused her to do so, not a sense of superiority. He continued to speak pleasantly. 'We have to make certain of all the facts, negatively as well as positively.'

'So your detective-inspector said.'

'Then I should be safe in repeating it.'

Reluctantly, her manner unfroze. 'All right, it's no fault of yours and you're only doing as you're told; and I really shouldn't fly off the handle at you as I just have.'

'I've broad shoulders, Mrs Tourkville . . . And as a matter of fact, I didn't come here to have a word with him, but with you.'

She was once more coldly antagonistic. 'I don't see how I can possibly help you.'

'By confirming that Mr Tourkville slept here every night last month.'

'Yes, he did.'

'He wasn't away a single night?'

'He was not.'

He was sad because she was lying.

★   ★   ★

Noyes stood in the middle of the courtyard behind the station and jingled some coins in his trouser pocket. How to prove Tourkville had been away from Highland Place the previous month and how to discover where he'd been? Useless to go back and question him, his wife, or either of the two farmhands again . . . He remembered what an old sergeant had once told him. 'It's a funny thing about human nature, but if you want to make a man do something he won't like doing, first threaten him with much worse;

174

then when that doesn't happen, he'll be so relieved he'll do what you want without arguing.' Subtly adapted . . .

★   ★   ★

The uniform PC was nearing the end of his probationary period and very conscious of the fact. He did everything by the book, even to the extent of signalling that he was turning left when he knew there was no traffic behind him.

Ada opened the front door of Highland Place and reluctantly let him into the hall. As he waited, he wondered just how much it cost a year to run a place like this? A sight more than he earned, that was for sure.

Tourkville, dressed for the fields except that he was wearing slippers, came into the hall. He spoke belligerently. 'What is it now? Do you have to keep bothering us? My wife says you were here only this morning?'

'Not me, sir.'

'One of you. Surely to God we've made it clear that neither of us can help? We did not see him a year ago, full stop.'

'I'm sorry, sir, but I don't know what you're talking about.' The PC, slightly awed by his surroundings and flustered by Tourkville's manner, spoke plaintively.

'Aren't you here because of Harwood?'

'No, sir.'

175

'Then why are you?'

'Because of the accident last month in Leicester.'

'What accident?'

'When your car was in collison with a light van. I'm sorry to have to tell you that the other driver is still in hospital.' He brought out a notebook from his pocket.

'I haven't had an accident.'

He turned the pages of his notebook, found the one he wanted, spoke in a monotonous tone. 'On the seventeenth of May at seven-five in the morning there was an accident at the junction of Spears Road and Waycroft Avenue, in the city of Leicester. The two vehicles involved were a Volvo shooting-brake and a Transit van. In a statement made by you . . .'

'I haven't been in Leicester in years and I haven't had an accident with a Transit van.'

Charlotte entered the hall. 'Is something wrong, Pierre?' As convinced as he had been initially that the PC was there because of the murder of Harwood, she was both scared and defiant.

Tourkville spoke with exasperation. 'He says I was in a car accident last month in Leicester.'

'But that's ridiculous.'

'Quite. But there's a problem in communicating.'

'When's it supposed to have been?'

176

'The seventeeth; early morning.'

She thought for a moment. 'That's when you were in Oxford for the club AGM.'

'At seven-five am . . .' began the PC.

Tourkville cut in. 'I was at the Brent Valley Motel, probably getting ready to eat breakfast.'

The PC decided that it needed more experienced heads than his to take this any further.

*   *   *

'The Brent Valley Motel at Oxford,' said Noyes.

'Oxford? That's not exactly next door to Etrington,' commented Burrow.

'Fair enough, Sarge, it isn't. But that doesn't matter, does it, not with a car handy. When Harwood was murdered, Tourkville wasn't at Highland Place as he claimed.'

'It still . . .'

'We're not trying to present a case in court. All we have to do is to persuade a magistrate that we should be granted an order to examine all his bank statements.'

Burrow was about to remind him that to slant the several pieces of evidence as he intended was contrary to the ethical standards of police work. But then he checked himself. As was so often the case, the means could be shown to justify the ends. Accept that the

177

evidence was still too equivocal to justify applying for an order to examine Tourkville's accounts, then no progress could be made; slant—not alter—the evidence so that it became strong enough to persuade a magistrate to grant the order and the accounts could be examined and it should be possible to decide whether or not Tourkville had been subjected to blackmail. If he had not, then it was likely, lacking any other motive, that any apparent involvement in the crime was merely coincidental. So what one was suggesting was going to prove his innocence, if innocent. To put it another way, it was in his own interests for the order to be made . . .

CHAPTER SEVENTEEN

Normally, the task of finding a person after forty-five years, especially with the commonest of all names, was rightly regarded as one of the most difficult and frustrating—people moved, married, and moved again. But Smith had never married and he still lived in the back-to-back house in Portsmouth in which he'd been born. It did not take the police long to find him.

'Are you the Smith who was on the *Waitawea* during the last war?' asked the uniform PC.

As he held on to the door for support, Smith sucked in his lower lip and chewed on it with his toothless gums.

'Well, were you?'

'What if I was?'

'Then I'd like a bit of a chat.'

The house stank of dirt, tom cat, and sickness. The dirt was ubiquitous, the neutered tom cat hostile, and Smith very ill. He'd obviously once been a large man, but now his back was bowed, his flesh looked like old putty, the top of his bald head was dotted with blotches of brown, his eyes were watery, and his hands trembled.

The PC sat on a chair, hoping it wasn't quite as filthy as it looked. 'You were on the *Waitawea* when she got torpedoed, right?'

'Yes.'

'And not many of you survived?'

'Four.'

'Who were the other three?'

'Johnny.'

'Johnny who?'

'Harwood.'

The PC said, speaking briskly because this might be bad news: 'I expect you've heard he died recently?' To his relief, Smith nodded. 'Who were the other two?'

'There was a cadet.'

'D'you remember his name?'

He shook his head.

'And the fourth man?'

179

'He was a seaman.'

'What was his name?'

For a while it seemed he wasn't going to answer, then he said, his tone changed: 'Andrews.'

The PC said curiously: 'What was it like in the boat?'

For the first time, Smith stared at the PC directly. 'You wouldn't understand,' he said with sudden contempt.

The PC was riled. 'How d'you know?'

'Because you wouldn't.'

'Come on, what was it like?'

Smith's vocabulary was limited and his powers of description poor, but strangely, these deficiencies had the effect of painting a far starker picture than might have been the case had he been more imaginative. The PC learned something of the courage that was called for if a man were to survive the tropical sun, the agonizing lack of water, and the constant presence of death.

'The four of you was lucky, then, to keep on going for several days after the captain died.'

'Was we?'

Life could be a real bastard, thought the PC. Smith had survived that hell only to reach his present one. 'You and Harwood must have seen quite a bit of the cadet before the ship was torpedoed?'

'Johnny used to serve him in the saloon.'

180

'What about outside the meals—surely you were with him pretty often?'

'With him an officer—or a kind of a one?'

'Was there ever any trouble between him and Harwood?'

'Why should there be?'

'I don't know; just wondered.'

'There weren't no trouble. And when the old man made the cadet sit at a table on his own, Johnny gave him extra grub.'

'Because he liked the cadet?'

'Because he hated the old man, like everyone else did.'

The PC dismissed that information as irrelevant. 'What about once you were in the boat—was there any trouble then between Harwood and the cadet?'

'Trouble? There was enough trouble with dying, wasn't there?'

The PC had been told to find out what was the nature of the relationship which had existed between Cadet Tourkville and Steward Harwood. It seemed that, in the normal sense of the word, there hadn't been a relationship.

★   ★   ★

Jenkins dropped the typewritten report on to his desk. 'This is from Portsmouth. Tourkville and Harwood had nothing to do with each other outside mealtimes. And if anything, Harwood quite liked Tourkville—he made certain the cadet had extra grub when the captain banished him to a table on his own; even if Harwood's prime motive seems to have been to say what he thought of the captain.'

'Why did the captain do that?' asked Noyes.

'How would I know?'

'Then what about once they were in the boat?'

'No trouble between Harwood and Tourkville. Which makes sense. Since they were dying by degrees, you wouldn't expect 'em to have a fifteen-round punch-up, would you?'

'So if Harwood was blackmailing Tourkville, we still have no idea why. Maybe we never will.'

'Then the case won't go to court.'

'You don't think so, sir?'

'I damn well know so. Much of the evidence is circumstantial or ambiguous. A strong, provable motive for the murder would cut out most of the ambiguities and tie down the circumstances . . . But if nothing ever happened between 'em, what gave grounds for blackmail?'

'Which kind of brings us round in a circle and leaves us jammed up our own exhaust pipe.'

'Sometimes, I find your sense of humour

182

bloody awful.'

'So does my wife.'

Jenkins pushed back his chair as he stood, crossed to the window and stared out. 'If Tourkville's innocent, why did he deny and go on denying that he knew Harwood?'

'He said . . .'

'I know what he said and it's a load of cod's. Just as it's a load that he did not meet Harwood a year ago. Why lie when a man of his upbringing and background can be expected to give all the help possible, unless he's scared that the connection will incriminate him?'

Noyes did not try to answer. Fingers crossed, he thought, that the accountant's report would force Tourkville to start giving answers.

*   *   *

The firm of accountants which the police used had their offices in a building in the centre of the redeveloped area just south of Watlingham's high street. The senior partner was in his middle fifties, distinguished-looking, and over-fond of gambling, a fact which had not yet come to the attention of his wife. ''Afternoon, Inspector.' He nodded at Noyes. Once everyone was seated, he opened a folder. 'We've examined all bank accounts, both private and farm, and the joint account

183

with the Abbey National Building Society. While I hasten to make the usual proviso that we cannot be certain of the facts unless we have the opportunity to question Mr Tourkville personally, the following would appear to be the position. Approximately one year ago, he drew five thousand pounds in cash; five months after that he drew a thousand pounds in cash and this was repeated every month until now, with one exception; these amounts are over and above all normal expenses.'

'Is there any regularity about the dates?'

'The five consecutive ones occurred at the beginning of each month.'

'And which month was the exception?'

'No cheque was drawn at the beginning of this one.'

'In practical terms, has this "missing" eleven thousand had any adverse effects?'

'There is a heavy overdraft, which mainly represents the purchase price of a farm. The interest on that overdraft has not been fully met and there has been no repayment of capital, as was originally agreed.'

'Then presumably the bank's been shouting?'

'I would expect the manager to have spoken to Mr Tourkville; obviously, I've no actual knowledge of the matter.'

'If a hundred thousand were "missing", would the estate be in real trouble?'

184

'Capital would have to be realized—presumably by selling land.'

'And with prices depressed, that would add up to a fair acreage?'

'Indeed.'

There were few other questions to be asked and the detectives left a couple of minutes later. They were walking through a shopping arcade when Jenkins said: 'Do you remember what you suggested?'

'In what way, sir?' asked Noyes carefully.

'If an accountant's investigation could be forced, Tourkville would be pinned down and would have to start answering questions.'

'Well, I thought . . .'

'The first DI I served under always said that he preferred his juniors not to think.'

They left the shopping arcade and turned left. Because there were few pedestrians, Jenkins deemed it judicious to discuss the case in detail. 'A thousand quid a month and no payment this month make it as plain as a pikestaff that Tourkville was being blackmailed up to, but not including, this month; which fits in precisely with Harwood being the blackmailer. But over the past year Harwood has spent up to a hundred thousand. Where the hell's the rest of the money come from?'

'A second blackmail.'

'That might be a reasonable answer if it didn't ignore something.'

185

'I hadn't forgotten . . .'

'If it didn't ignore the fact that everything we've uncovered so far limits the base of the blackmail to the last voyage of the *Waitawea*. Since there were four survivors, only three men can possibly be concerned in Harwood's death. Smith is terminally ill and Andrews was killed in the penultimate year of the war, which leaves Tourkville.' They reached the entrance to the courtyard at the back of the station and Jenkins came to a stop. 'So what's the answer?'

CHAPTER EIGHTEEN

Tourkville and Doyle stood at the top of the sloping field. 'Vines?' said Doyle in tones of incredulity.

'That's what I'm thinking of. You must have read that in the past thirty or so years quite a number of vineyards have been planted in the southern half of the country.'

'I've also read that they get killed by the rain, killed by the frosts, killed by the hail, and killed by the pox.'

It seemed, thought Tourkville, that Doyle, an arch traditionalist, credited a vine with nearly as many lives as a cat, not to mention his confusion between phylloxera and syphilis.

186

'This field grows the best early grass of any,' Doyle said.

'I know it's pretty good . . .'

'And it's the first to graze, being so well drained and the ground never puddling. The stock's out here a month before anywhere else.'

'Surely not as much as a month?'

'A month,' Doyle repeated firmly.

'Maybe we could get the corner field to come in earlier if we dug the ditch deeper and mole-ploughed more regularly?'

'Never.'

'Well, it's only an idea at the moment. But I did think it would be fun to be able to drink our own wine throughout the year.' Doyle liked wine and his Christmas present always included three bottles of Rioja.

'The early bullocks wouldn't never do as well.'

Tourkville looked at his watch. 'I'd better be getting back to the house; we've some people coming along at ten-thirty.'

Doyle stared down the field. 'Vines!' He tried to sound as contemptuous as before, but failed. There was no doubt that the thought of being able to drink wine throughout the year was an attractive one.

Tourkville turned and walked up to the nearest gateway. No longer able to concern his mind with estate matters, his previous fears returned. Why had the police obtained a court order to investigate his bank acounts? Had they learned anything from the figures?

By the time he reached the house, Arkwell had arrived and, with Charlotte, was in the larger sitting-room, a room of rather too much pomp for modern taste. Younger than Tourkville, he looked older; his speech was frequently pedantic and his manners possessed a punctiliousness which spoke of past days, as did his invariable dress of black coat and striped trousers. His firm, of which he was now senior partner, had handled the Tourkville family's legal matters for generations.

Seven minutes later, Jenkins and Noyes arrived. They were offered coffee, but Jenkins declined for them both, giving Noyes no chance to accept.

'As you know,' said Jenkins, 'we obtained a court order permitting up to examine your bank accounts.'

Arkwell spoke in his plummy voice that was so redolent of a good Graham's. 'My client is only too well aware of that fact. He wishes to say that he is totally unable to understand why any such order should have been sought, let alone executed.'

'Perhaps if I detail certain facts, things will become clear . . . Mr Tourkville, over the past few weeks, initially at the request of the Etrington police, we have been investigating the circumstances surrounding the murder of

John Harwood, with whom you sailed in the *Waitawea*. These investigations suggest that the motive for the murder may very well have been to stop him continuing a blackmail. When we asked you if you'd been blackmailed, you denied it. I'd like to put the same question again.'

'My client utterly denies the absurd allegation,' said Arkwell.

'I would prefer it if Mr Tourkville answered.'

'No doubt. however, we will continue as we have begun.'

'You don't think it might be in his interests, if innocent, to establish the facts as quickly and as directly as possible?'

'Your question carries a connotation which you are not entitled to introduce. The fact that my client chooses to answer your questions through me cannot begin to be construed as any indication of guilt.'

'Of course not,' agreed Jenkins easily. He nodded at Noyes, who passed him a small director's case. He opened the lid and brought out two sheets of paper. 'Our accountant has examined all your bank accounts and building society account, Mr Tourkville. I'm afraid that I'm not up to explaining how he reached his conclusions, but should you want to know this he is, of course, authorized to give you any specific details you ask for.'

189

'Required, not authorized,' observed Arkwell.

Jenkins smiled briefly. 'The only point I'm trying to make is that you can accept my figures as being correct.'

'My client accepts no such thing. His reason for agreeing to this meeting was to learn on what grounds you applied to the court for the order to examine his financial afairs.'

'Put very roughly, it was to discover whether he had paid out sums of money over and above normal expenses.'

'And if he had?'

'That would suggest he was being blackmailed.'

'It would suggest no such thing.'

Jenkins waited, then said: 'A year ago, Mr Tourkville, you drew five thousand pounds in cash; for the past six months—that's not including this one—you have drawn a thousand pounds in cash at the beginning of each month. Why was this money drawn?'

'Because my client wished to draw it,' said Arkwell.

'I'll rephrase my question. For what purpose was the money needed?'

'Various expenses.'

'For the five years prior to the first date in question, your general outgoings were consistent, your particular ones exactly specified. Then this sum of five thousand was drawn. What particular expense did that meet?'

'Not one expense,' said Arkwell, 'but many, all of a general nature.'

'Could you detail them?'

'There is no call to be specific.'

'At the beginning of this month, you did not withdraw a thousand pounds in cash, as you had the six previous months; had an expense, or expenses, suddenly ceased?'

'And if it had?'

Jenkins sighed. 'We're not going to get very far like this, Mr Arkwell. Surely your client would like to help us clear up the matter as soon as possible? Normally, an innocent man is only too keen . . .'

'I have already objected to your suggesting that in order to underline his innocence, my client must answer your questions.'

'Yes, you have. Did Harwood visit you here about a year ago?'

'My client has never received a visit from Harwood.'

'And if an independent witness testified that one day, roughly half a mile from here, Harwood asked him where Highland Place was?'

'If that witness is Thompson, sacked for theft, he clearly is far from being "independent".'

'When did you last see Harwood?'

'My client last saw and spoke to him on

191

that day, forty-five years ago, when they were landed in the United Kingdom, in the company of the two other survivors.'

'What was your relationship with Harwood?'

'My client's relationship with him was precisely what was to be expected as existing between a cadet and a saloon steward.'

'What was your relationship with Harwood in the boat?'

'What the hell d'you think it was?' said Tourkville wildly.

'It would be much better . . .' began Arkwell.

'When you're burned black and dying, do you imagine there are specific, analysable relationships?'

'But something happened in that boat, didn't it?' persisted Jenkins.

'We bloody died . . .'

★   ★   ★

Men died. And it seemed as if there were as many ways of dying as there were men to die. There was the stoker who stood, said 'Goodbye', and stepped over the gunwhale; they watched him drift slowly astern, his corn-coloured hair spread out by the green-blue sea which slowly heaved to distant storms. There was the DEMS rating who was saying that when he reached land he was going to enter the first pub and drink it dry who suddenly collapsed to the boards, already dead. There was the steward who went into delirium and for hour after hour called on God to save him; just before he died, he screamed blasphemies at the god who had betrayed him. There was the steward who died with a knife in his stomach, bewildered by the irony of a violent death in the middle of a lingering one. There was the stoker who fell over the side during the night and shrieked with fear because he couldn't swim; as the hull slid past, he managed to grab one of the after lifelines looped along the side; he called on them to drag him back aboard, but try as they did, they couldn't lift him. Later, now quite silent, he let go of the line and drifted away. There was the seaman who went mad and had to be pinioned with rope and who repeatedly 'saw' a rescuing craft; each time, the other survivors knew momentary hope, even though they also knew him to be mad and suffering from hallucinations . . .

It was conventional wisdom that the man who had much to live for would last longer than the man who did not. This proved to be false; or at least it seemed to be proved to be false. Who truly knew what each man had to live for but that man?—and when he was dead he could not say. The seaman with blond hair had a wife and year-old daughter and he loved them both so much that he never went ashore in foreign ports because then he could allot his wife a greater proportion of his pay. He died on the third day. On his last leave in Aberdeen, the fireman had found his wife in bed with a flight lieutenant. Instead of being ashamed, she'd screamed at him that every time he was away at sea she lowered her pants for any man who took her fancy. He lasted until the nineteenth day . . .

Rank commanded even when it was obvious it would, or could, not command. The captain continued to live in a different world, but the survivors instinctively looked to him for their salvation. The bos'un, small, chunky, battered, as tough as a steak from a fighting bull, issued orders in the name of the captain. When the bos'un died, Andrews did the same, but in him there was a malicious acknowledgement of the charade. When the captain died, Tourkville became ranking officer and so now the orders were channelled through him . . .

★   ★   ★

'Why was the steward knifed?' asked Jenkins.

Tourkville, his expression drawn, was miles away; it was several seconds before he answered. 'He'd stolen water.'

'Who knifed him?'

'No one ever knew.'

'You all must have done, in a lifeboat in which no one could move without everyone else being aware of the fact.'

'All right. No one bloody cared. There were thirty-five of us in the beginning—more than either of the other two boats because we had the engine. The engine didn't work and so all it really meant was less space. Thirty-five in a boat smaller than that carpet.'

They stared at the Persian carpet. It was virtually impossible for them to visualize thirty-five men crammed together in a space smaller than that.

'There were two water tanks slung under thwarts; each one held fifteen gallons. Less than a gallon a man with no one knowing how many days it was going to have to last. The bos'un fixed the ration at one ladle in the morning, one at midday, and one at night. After the third day, all that ladle of water seemed to do was make the agony more acute, but every minute of every hour was lived for the next ration . . . One night the steward was caught stealing water. But that wasn't why he was knifed.'

'No?' said the inspector, astonished.

'He'd just dipped the ladle into the tank and it was full. In trying to move away quickly, to hide what he'd been doing, he let the ladle tip up and we heard the water splashing into the bilge; water which any one

195

of us would have sold his soul to drink.'

'Oh my God!' whispered Charlotte.

'Could Harwood have killed him?' asked the inspector.

'Good God, no!'

'Why not?'

'That sort of thing wasn't in him; far too effete. Before it all happened, I'd have given odds he'd have been the first to go.'

'Do you know, then, why he survived?'

'Because Daisy kept kicking him back into life.'

'You had a woman in the boat?

'Daisy was the nickname for Smith, the other half of the partnership. An enormous bull of a man, as strong as an ox and not even scared of death.'

'When did the last man die?'

'I don't remember, exactly; it'll probably be in the log.'

'Do you have that log here?'

Tourkville shook his head. 'I handed it to the company when we landed and later on they presented it to the Merchant Navy Museum in Plaistow.'

'You never told me that,' said Charlotte.

'I wanted to forget,' he said fiercely.

'Who was the last person to die?' asked Jenkins.

She swung round. 'What's it matter who it was? Why d'you go on and on? Can't you see what you're doing to him? Haven't you understood a single word of what it was like for him?'

'I can understand, but still not know,' replied Jenkins quietly. 'The real horror can only be appreciated by someone who experienced it. If I possibly could, I would drop the subject; unfortunately, it's my duty not to.'

'My client has explained in great detail . . .' began Arkwell.

'Bear with me just a little longer . . . Mr Tourkville, who was the last man to die?'

'The captain.'

'You've said you can't remember exactly when he did die, can you give me some sort of approximation?'

Tourkville was silent.

'Was it one day, two days, or more before you were picked up?'

'Nine or ten.'

'When he died, you were in command?'

'Only because I wore epaulettes. It was Andrews who brought us through. Even Daisy had begun to give up, but he forced us to go on fighting. He . . .' He stopped.

'He what?'

Tourkville shook his head.

'Stop it,' said Charlotte.

Jenkins looked at her. 'You're right, Mrs Tourkville.' He stood.

Arkwell said pompously: 'You are satisfied now that my client is quite unable to help you?'

'Shall we say, I've no further questions to put to him at the moment.'

CHAPTER NINETEEN

'It's a funny world,' said Jenkins.

It's also a bloody dangerous one, thought Noyes, as they overtook on a blind corner.

'You meet someone, use your experience to size him up and categorize him, would wager a fortune you could detail his stereotyped life, and then discover you couldn't be more wrong if you tried.'

'Makes a difference, learning just how much he went through.'

'A difference in what way?'

'You've got to feel some sympathy for him.'

'Even if he was a murderer?'

'Harwood had a record and then moved out of his class and into blackmail.'

'Which in your book makes him expendable?'

'I'm not saying that. I'm just saying . . . It's difficult to put into words. But it's something like that when you know the truth the blacks and whites aren't nearly so easy to distinguish from each other.'

'They seldom are. But do we yet know the

truth; have we learned anything fresh this morning?'

'Not to go to sea.'

'Dammit!' snapped Jenkins, as he braked sharply to avoid ramming a light van. 'I've told you before, leave your sense of humour at home.'

'Yes, sir.'

'Now answer the question. Have we discovered anything fresh?'

'Thanks to that pompous old basket, Arkwell, not really.'

'Did he play such a negative part as all that? Every time he prevented Tourkville answering a question, he was suggesting that the answer could be damaging. Tourkville was clearly being blackmailed.'

'But the books say for eleven thousand, not for a hundred thousand.'

'So is there a source of money belonging to Tourkville we haven't uncovered?'

'If there were, wouldn't he have cut back the huge overdraft long since?'

'Businesses often prefer to work on borrowed money.'

'I don't see Tourkville doing that. He's too old-fashioned. You know, neither a borrower nor a lender be.'

'If he has no other source of money, if he was blackmailed but only for the eleven thousand, where did the very much larger amount of money come from?'

'Someone else who was being blackmailed.'

'We've decided that if we're right as to the grounds for blackmailing Tourkville, there can't be anyone else.'

'Why don't we just ship all the papers up to Etrington and let them worry?'

'For once, I'm inclined to agree with you.'

They were silent for a while. Then, as they drew to a halt at a crossroads which marked a village, Noyes said: 'If Etrington send the paper on to the DPP, d'you think he'll decide to prosecute Tourkville for the murder of Harwood?'

'I wouldn't like to bet either way.' Jenkins engaged first and accelerated across the road. 'Remember my saying there'd be a prosecution if and when a strong motive could be established? Blackmail's a strong enough one. But you don't need much imagination to work out what kind of a meal a good defence counsel would make of that discrepancy in the figures.'

★   ★   ★

'You must tell me,' said Charlotte. She had not moved from the chair.

'When I get back,' replied Tourkville. 'I promised George . . .'

'You must tell me now.'

He saw the expression on her face, went over and stood in front of the fireplace.

'What happened to the money? The bank's been creating trouble because nothing's been paid off; yet in the past eleven months you've drawn eleven thousand in cash. Where's it all gone?'

'Where I told them—general expenses.'

'Please, I'm not a fool. Is it . . .' She broke off, nibbled her lower lip, held her head a little higher. 'Have you found another woman?'

'What?'

'Have you found another woman who's giving you something I can't? If you have, for God's sake don't beat about the bush any longer, but tell me.'

'From the day we married, I've never touched another woman.'

'Thank God,' she murmured. She plucked at one of the buttons on her frock.

'You really thought I've been having an affair?'

'Pierre, can't you see? When the inspector talked about the eleven thousand . . . I know what the estate means to you; I know that one of the happiest moments of your life was when you bought Dower Farm. Yet you've drawn and spent eleven thousand pounds which should have gone to paying off the interest and capital and that's put so much at risk. If the bank pressed really hard, you'd have to sell land. And for you that would be a total disaster. Only something exceptional would make you risk it. Who or what can that be, if not another woman?'

He stared through the middle of the three windows at the garden and the rolling countryside beyond. In the face of such beauty, the truth became even more disgusting . . .

'Tell me. Whatever it is, it won't make any difference to my love for you.'

★   ★   ★

The lugsail had been blown out and repeatedly rent in a series of short, fierce wind squalls which, with merciless irony, brought them no rain. They used the pieces of canvas as best they could to provide shade, but with little success. Their bodies were burned almost from head to foot and the salt increased the agony. But even that pain was as nothing compared to the pain of thirst; this savaged their bodies and their minds. And those who could still think with any clarity knew that their ration of water, already reduced to two ladles a day, would shortly have to be reduced to one; after that, it could not be long before the last of them died and the boat was manned by rotting corpses.

Two hours after a greaser died—it took them over an hour to manage to tip his body over the side—they were suddenly surrounded by gambolling fish that seemed fascinated by the drifting boat, repeatedly circling it. At first, no one took any notice of them, being far too deeply sunk in pain. But then Andrews, after watching them for a long while, said to the captain that they must catch as many of them as they possibly could. The captain, his* brick-red face pitted with suppurating sores, made no reply, indeed gave no indication that he had understood. Andrews called on Tourkville to give him a hand and together they moved for'd—it was not difficult now since there were only twelve survivors—and after a long struggle they unscrewed the circular lid of the metal locker slung under the for'd thwart. Packed inside were highly nutritious biscuits and chocolate—it was days since anyone had eaten—several fishing lines with different sized hooks, to each of which was attached a coloured lure, two bags, one solid, the other made with a small mesh, a knife, and a pamphlet of instructions, printed on rubberized linen, which explained how to cut up a fish and squeeze the flesh in order to obtain a liquid that was perfectly drinkable and nutritious.

They streamed the lines. The fish ignored the lures. A seaman, his curses virtually inaudible because his voice was now less than a croak, threw his line into the sea; a steward wound in his line and caught the palm of his right hand on a triple hook—for a long time, he merely stared at the lightly embedded hook and made no attempt to free it.

The fish stayed with them throughout the day and although Andrews, Tourkville, and a greaser, streamed the lines until dark, they caught nothing.

The fish were still there next morning, seeming to mock the survivors. Two men had died during the night. Those left who still had some strength were about to begin the struggle to tip the bodies over the side, when Andrews stopped them.

He faced the captain. 'We've got to catch some fish,' he croaked.

The captain said nothing.

'Pull yourself together, you stupid old bastard; you're meant to be in command.' It was the first time anyone had put into words the scorn and hatred all of them felt for the man who had betrayed them.

The captain might not have heard.

Andrews spoke to Tourkville. 'We must catch fish. If they won't take the lures, we'll use bait.'

Until they began to collect the bait, Tourkville had not realized what it was to be. When he did, he knew surprise rather than revulsion.

They threaded the pieces of flesh on to hooks and then trailed two lines. The first strike came within a minute, the second almost immediately afterwards. Ironically, since he was the stronger, it was Andrews who lost his line as it was plucked out of his grip by the force of the strike; perhaps his fish had been much larger than the one on Tourkville's line.

It took them five minutes to haul in and land the three-foot dorado. They cut it up into cubes, put several of these into the net bag, and twisted this with all their strength over the second, solid bag. There was a thin trickle of pinkish liquid. They discarded those cubes, dropped fresh ones into the mesh bag. The one fish gave each of the twelve a drink.

They caught four more fish before, with shocking suddenness, they all disappeared. One moment the sea was alive with them, the next there was none. They continued to stream their lines, but all they saw was the fin of a cruising shark . . .

*   *   *

'You had to do it,' she said fiercely.

'Is that what people at home would have said?'

'Yes.'

'I doubt it. They'd have been revolted.'

She stood, crossed to the chair in which he now sat, put her arms round him and rested her cheek against his. 'Only the fools. The two men were dead and you were going to throw their bodies overboard; the fish would have eaten them just the same.'

'But people wouldn't have seen things with such cold logic.'

'In such ghastly circumstances, ordinary values no longer apply. Pierre, why can't you accept that? You had to do what you did.'

'I haven't finished.'

She had not listened. 'I don't care what anyone says, you had to do it. Look at what happens all the time—lungs, livers, kidneys, even hearts, are taken and transplanted into other people to save their lives. Where's the difference?'

'For one thing, there weren't transplants back in those days and so people weren't conditioned to the idea.'

'But it's now that they'd hear what had happened. Why didn't you tell me all this long ago? I could have made you understand how wrong it was to give in to that foul little man and let him blackmail you—he did blackmail you, didn't he?'

'I haven't finished.'

This time, she had listened. She drew in her breath sharply. She came round the side of the chair, sat on his lap—something she had not done for more years than she could remember—and pressed against him as tightly as she could, trying to reassure as she sought reassurance. She was very scared.

206

There were just five survivors now; the captain, Tourkville, Andrews, Harwood, and Smith. Despite the room there was in the boat, they huddled together in the stern, afraid to die alone.

For some time there'd been a force three to four wind and the light sea, crossing a long swell, slapped against the hull, occasionally raising a spray which splattered them. The sky was clear and the ferocious sun burned their already burned flesh.

Tourkville struggled to hold the pencil firmly enough to write in his log, a soft-covered exercise book. Initially, the entries had been frequent, full, and lucid, now they were occasional, brief, disjointed, and in parts illegible. He didn't know why he still kept a log; who would there be to read it?

'Look!'

After a while, he realized that Andrews was pointing out to port. He slowly shifted his gaze.

'We must catch . . . but no bait,' said Andrews with painful slowness.

He could see nothing to catch. His mind drifted . . .

*   *   *

She whispered: 'Then what happened?'

'I don't know,' he replied hoarsely. 'It's just a blur. I've tried again and again to remember. Christ! I've tried—but I can't.'

'Then what did that beastly little man tell you?'

'That I said we had to kill the captain if any of us was to survive.'

She had come to realize that it had to be something like this, yet the words still provoked an immediate, shrill denial. 'No.'

'He said I killed him with a knife we'd used on the fish.'

'He was lying. The captain must have died naturally.'

'He was no nearer death than the rest of us.'

'That doesn't mean he couldn't die first.'

'If that's all that happened, why would my mind refuse to remember?'

'Because by then you were delirious. Pierre, I know you. You couldn't kill anyone.'

'When it's kill or die?'

'You'd fight and fight to survive, but you couldn't and wouldn't deliberately kill.'

'If he died, the four of us might live.'

'For you, could that have justified the killing of him?'

'I . . . I don't know.'

'Why won't you believe in yourself?'

'Because he'd made my life hell from the beginning of the trip and done everything to humiliate me. I'd cause enough to hate him.'

'That would never turn you into a murderer.'

'He'd betrayed everyone aboard. We'd nothing but contempt for him. It's easy to kill or condemn to death someone for whom you feel contempt.'

'No, it is not; not for someone of your character. Trust yourself instead of a foul little blackmailer.'

'But don't you understand? I can remember Andrews pointing and making out that the fish were back. But I looked and looked and couldn't see any. And Harwood said they never returned.'

CHAPTER TWENTY

Noyes made a third mistype, ripped out the C12 form from the typewriter, scrumpled it up and threw it at the waste-paper basket; it hit the side and fell to the floor.

'Temper, temper,' said the DC at the next desk.

Noyes wound a fresh C12 form into the typewriter. The internal telephone was on his desk and it rang after he'd typed no more than a couple of words. The desk sergeant told him that Mrs Tourkville was in the front room and requesting to speak to him.

The other DC had gathered enough from Noyes's end of the conversation to judge that a woman was waiting below. 'Is she a blonde?'

'Out of your class.'

'Look who's talking!'

He left and went down the stairs and along corridors to the front room. Charlotte Tourkville was seated at one of the low tables at the far end of the oblong room. He was shocked by her expression of distress.

She fiddled with her handbag as she stared up at him.

'I've come here to . . .' She stopped.

'Yes?'

She spoke in a rush. 'To ask you to find out the truth.'

'Just a moment.' He went across to the counter and found out from the duty sergeant which of the interview rooms was free. He led the way along a passage lit by overhead strip lights and into the first of the four.

Recently, it had been repainted in two shades of green and framed colour prints had been hung on the near wall on either side of the list of interviewee's rights, but any sense of informality these changes might have implemented was negated by the bars over the single small, high-up window.

She settled at the table. 'If I tell you something, will you promise not to pass it on to anyone else?'

'I'm sorry, but if what you tell me is connected with the case and is important, then I have to give the information to my superiors.'

'Just for once . . . ?'

'Mrs Tourkville, don't you think it would be best to go and talk things over with your solicitor first?'

'No.'

'I really would advise you . . .'

'Arkwell's so terribly conventional; he couldn't begin to realize . . . You're a fighter. If you believe in something, you'll fight and fight for it, won't you?'

'I'd like to think that's true.'

'Oh God, I wish I knew what to do. Suppose terrible suffering really can change a man out of character? After all, I've never believed that it ennobles; how can it, when it's cruel and horrible?'

He waited, not understanding what she was talking about, yet able to appreciate her mental agony at the need to come to a decision.

She finally said: 'I know I'm right. Nothing could change him so completely . . . You don't like my husband, do you?'

He was surprised and disconcerted by the question. 'I . . . I neither like nor dislike him.'

She ignored his denial. 'Is it because of the kind of person he is, or the position he

211

holds?'

'What does it matter?'

'It matters terribly. Which is it?'

He answered her unwillingly. 'His position, I suppose.'

'Then I can tell you . . . It's just as important to prove a man's innocence as his guilt, isn't it?'

'In many cases, yes.'

'Prove Pierre's innocence.'

He shook his head. 'I'm sorry, the case is out of our hands. All the evidence has been sent up to Etrington and it's entirely their pigeon now.'

'I'm not talking about the murder of Harwood. He couldn't have done that in a thousand years.'

'Then prove he is innocent of what?' he asked, bewildered.

She opened her handbag, brought out a slim cigarette case, and offered it. When he said he didn't smoke, she asked if he minded if she did. She lit a cigarette and greedily inhaled the smoke. 'I haven't smoked for years until the other day. When the medical reports made it clear how dangerous it is, Pierre gave it up and told me I must do the same. It wasn't nearly so easy for me. He's an iron willpower. People don't understand that when they just meet him casually. They don't realize that for years and years he worked himself almost into the ground to save the

212

estate, even though the experts said he was wasting his time.'

'I would imagine you worked as hard.'

'Because his dedication shamed me into doing so. He saw himself as owing a duty towards both the family that had gone and the family that was to come. It's because of this tremendous sense of where his duty lies that I'm so certain he couldn't have . . .'

He waited.

'Why should a mind deliberately forget?'

'I'm afraid I'm no expert on that sort of question. I suppose one answer could be that there'd be such distress if it remembered.'

'But you can't turn that round, can you, and say that if it has forgotten, it's because there must have been a series of events to cause such a distress?'

'No, of course not.'

'Terrible physical and mental stress on their own could be responsible?'

'I'm sure of that, yes . . . Mrs Tourkville, if all this has nothing to do with the death of Harwood, what does it have to do with?'

She looked at him so intently that he had the uncomfortable feeling that she was questioning his soul. 'Pierre believes he killed the captain.'

For a moment he looked blankly at her, then he said: 'You mean, the captain of the *Waitawea*?'

She spoke with breathless speed; in only

one respect did she alter what her husband had told her and that was to say that the fish had returned. She finished with a question. 'Suppose Harwood wasn't lying and Pierre did carry some responsibility for the captain's death, could he still he held to account?'

'Well, there's no statute of limitations for murder, so in theory if it could be proved now that the captain had been deliberately killed, those responsible could be tried.'

'He'd betrayed them all.'

'That's immaterial.'

'If he hadn't died, the others wouldn't have lived.'

'Necessity can never be a defence. That was established roughly a hundred years ago in a case . . .' He stopped. The case had concerned men adrift in a small boat who had turned to murder and cannibalism to survive.

'Would my husband be tried?'

'I said in theory he could be, but in practical terms—and please don't forget that I'm no expert on this—I doubt it. We're talking about something which happened a very long time ago, the only other known witness is a very sick man and quite possibly unwilling or unable to give evidence, and broadly speaking a confession has to be supported by independent facts because people do confess to crimes they have not committed. And even if I'm wrong on all that and he were charged, and found guilty, I

214

can't see a court being anything but lenient in view of his youth, inexperience, and the appalling hardships.'

'Then why . . .' She stopped.

'Why what?'

She shook her head. 'I know he could not have killed the captain or given the order to kill him. But he won't have as much faith in himself as I have in him . . . Please, please prove I'm right.'

★   ★   ★

Burrow brought out his pipe and rubbed the bowl against the palm of his left hand.

'So how do we go about proving it?' asked Noyes.

Burrow searched for his tobacco pouch. 'Damn, I seem to have left it at home! . . . Give me a fag.'

'I don't smoke.'

'Ever useless.' He put the pipe down on the desk. 'It's immaterial whether or not Tourkville killed the captain, or gave the order which was carried out by someone else. He was prepared to believe he might have done, paid out good money because of that, and therefore had every reason to want to shut Harwood up.'

'I'm talking about the captain's death.'

'We're not interested in that unless it seems a case can be brought—and I'd say you

215

summed up the situation to her accurately enough.'

'I promised her we'd try to uncover the truth.'

'Quite right. Keep the customer happy.'

'How the hell can you be so bloody cynical?'

'Look who's talking!' Burrow suddenly stood and went over to his mackintosh, from the right-hand pocket of which he brought a tobacco pouch. 'Just remembered,' he said with satisfaction, as he returned to his chair.

'Is that all you're concerned about?'

'A pipe of baccy helps to keep my blood pressure within bounds when I have to deal with a DC who's showing signs of losing his marbles.' He began to pack the bowl. 'You know, you're puzzling me. Why all the concern? I thought you couldn't stand Tourkville?'

'I can't stand what he represents; that's got nothing to do with the case.'

'You're finally beginning to learn.'

'I've learned he couldn't have killed, or have given the order to kill, the captain.'

Burrow struck a match and lit his pipe. 'Forget the captain. Someone murdered Harwood and the evidence says the motive was blackmail. No one other than Tourkville could have been blacked.'

'Are you so sure? Remember the discrepancy between the eleven thousand

216

pounds from Tourkville's accounts and the hundred thousand Harwood probably spent?'

'Of course.'

'Assume Tourkville doesn't have a Swiss bank account—and if he did, surely he'd have drawn the eleven thousand from it—where did the rest of the money come from?'

'In the circumstances, it's too big an assumption to make, despite your caveat.' He tamped down the burning tobacco with the base of his lighter.

'Why not make it all the same? Then the answer's obvious—one of the dead isn't dead.'

'If I had a bit more imagination, I'd say you're as tight as two ticks.'

'What kind of a man was Andrews?'

'The seaman who survived, only to get blown up by a V-2?' Burrow thought for a while. 'A smart alec, from all accounts; the kind of bloke you find in every service—clever enough to know just how insolent he can get without being clobbered.'

'That, Sarge, and more. He was quick-thinking and quick-acting; he saved the boat from being tipped end up when something caught. He had all the drive and determination; when the bos'un died, he took command, though always in the name of authority—the captain or Tourkville. Even at sixteen-and-a-half, on his first trip, Tourkville held the captain in contempt; in how much greater contempt must Andrews have held him? When a smart, hard, intelligent, determined man holds someone in contempt, he often regards him as totally expendable . . . What I'm saying is that it's probable the captain was killed and did not die from thirst and exposure because Andrews judged that by his death the rest of them might live, while if he lived on much longer, they'd all inevitably die; Andrews used Tourkville's rank as cover for his own decision. Tourkville was virtually delirious by then and remembers nothing of the murder—perhaps because of the state he was in, but perhaps also because he knew that since he was *de jure* in command he should have prevented it and therefore it was easier for him if his mind deliberately flipped.'

'You've been doing quite a bit of thinking around this one.'

'That's right. So now you do some. Look at circumstances as they were after the rescue as Andrews would have seen them. There were three eye-witnesses to what had happened. The two stewards and Tourkville. The stewards came from poor backgrounds and like as not normally their sympathies would lie with a criminal rather than with justice; in this case, that's where they must lie because they owed their lives to the crime. Tourkville however, was a different kettle of fish. His background was privilege and the rich always favour the law because that's what preserves their privilege. At sixteen-and-a-half, he couldn't be mentally tough and although it seemed he'd no memory of the final events, that memory might return and then his conscience and training would force him to speak up, even though by doing so he must inevitably place himself in a situation inimical, if not downright dangerous, to himself. So Andrews decided he'd got to vanish. My guess is he returned to sea, satisfied that in the fog of war he'd be 'lost' long enough to find a way of disappearing permanently. Then, on a leave, he was very close to a V-2 incident and here was his chance in the shape of a body so shattered that identification could only be by papers.'

Burrow flicked open his lighter and relit his pipe. Once it was well alight and belching out smoke, he said: 'You even make it sound plausible.'

'It's what happened, more or less.'

The acrid smoke began to disperse throughout the room because, ever cold, Burrow had kept the window shut. 'Suppose you're right, then Andrews is now in a position to have paid somewhere between seventy and ninety thousand quid in blackmail—he's feathered his own nest to some tune.'

'Why not? He's made for business—sharp, hard, and totally unscrupulous.'

219

'Tell me something. Haven't you ever met a pleasant capitalist?'

'A contradiction in terms . . . So we start looking for Andrews, right?'

'Just like that? A different name, over forty years back, making certain he's had no point of contact with his old identity, as rich as Crœsus and using his money as a shield? Try finding the pot of gold at the end of the rainbow, it'll be a lot easier. You put in a report to Etrington and leave them with the facts—and if I were you, I'd keep them simple.'

'I promised Mrs Tourkville we'd try to find the truth about the captain's death.'

'Then you'd better unpromise her.' His pipe had gone out and he stared at it with sharp annoyance.

'Sarge, we must help her . . .'

'How many cases have you sitting on your desk right now?'

'I haven't counted.'

'Then go and do it and you'll find you need your toes as well as your fingers. All cases which concern crimes committed here and now, not a maybe crime committed before either of us was born.'

'What kind of a hell d'you think she's going through right now, not knowing the truth?'

'What kind of hell are the people going through who're connected with the cases on your desk?'

'I want to try and find Andrews.'

'Only in your free time.'

Noyes stared at the detective-sergeant for several seconds, then he said: 'I've ten days' leave due.'

'Well?'

'I want to take it now.'

'You know the regulations. At least three weeks' notice of intention . . .'

'You've worked it often enough before now. The old man doesn't know whether or not I gave you notice three weeks back.'

Burrow scratched his cheek with the stem of the pipe. 'What's the attraction? Has she offered you a small fortune to try and clear her husband?'

'No, she bloody hasn't.'

'No need to take off, just asking. And wondering.'

'What?'

'What it is in even an elderly woman that gets a man running?'

CHAPTER TWENTY-ONE

'I've been rather extravagant,' said Carol.

Noyes put their empty sherry glasses down by the side of the sink. 'That's OK by me just so long as you made certain the bill comes to you.'

'I bought a leg of lamb for supper.'

'You've taken out a second mortgage on the house?'

'Lamb was on offer at the butcher's. We seem to have been eating lash-ups for weeks and when I saw all the legs in the window, I could feel myself eating one.'

'You should have looked a little longer and you wouldn't have needed to buy.'

'But then you'd have gone hungry . . . I did wonder whether the sudden yen meant I'm preggers.'

'What's that?'

'What would you do if I were?'

'Sue the firm which made the pills.'

'But would you be glad?'

He hesitated, then said: 'Damned if I know.'

'At least that's honest . . . I expect you'd be glad, once you'd got used to the idea. Under that hard exterior, there does beat a heart.' She walked over and kissed him lightly on the cheek. 'You can take that worried look off your face. In fact, it was pure greed, not a strange pregnant desire . . . In honour of Larry the Lamb, we'll eat in the dining-room and you can wait on me to add a touch of class.'

He grinned at her, went through to the dining-room. When she talked like that, it seemed to restore to their relationship much of the simple, amusing, yet deep love with which, as he now remembered, it had started.

They had finished the first course and were clearing the table when he was reminded that, whatever his memory now said, no human relationship was ever simple.

'I popped into Campbell's, the travel agents, on my way back because one of their posters in the window gave me another yen,' she said, as she loaded the tray.

'Did that suggest twins?'

She laughed. 'The poster said that it's always sunny in Tenerife.'

'I expect you could get them under the Trades Description Act for that.'

'I don't know so much. There was an article recently in one of the papers which said that the Canaries have the perfect climate. I went inside and asked if there were any week holidays still going and there are. Just talking about all that sun made me want to strip off.'

'Presumably, the young man behind the counter was very suave?'

'He was a she . . . It really would be wonderful to get away for a week. So let's book.'

Because he had been going along with her frothy sense of fun, he had not stopped to realize what she was leading up to. She did not miss his change of expression. 'You said you were owed time off.'

223

'Yes, but . . .' If he forgot his promise to Charlotte Tourkville, and his quixotic decision to use part of his leave to try to uncover the truth, if he now said 'Book', then the laughter would return. If he didn't, he could be certain that Carol would be bitterly disappointed and the evening which had started as such fun would end as had so many in the past months. Why sacrifice his own happiness for someone to whom he owed no responsibility; even more to the point, to someone who came from a background he had always despised? Then he remembered the depths of Charlotte Tourkville's despair and knew he must honour his pledge. 'The work's been piling up so fast it's almost buried me. The old man said there could be no leave for anyone until we've cleared up the backlog.'

'Do they or don't they owe you leave?'

'Yes, but as I've just said . . .'

'Then they can't deny you what's due to you.'

'I've told you before, in the CID it's always a case of give and take . . .'

'That's a dirty joke which isn't even blue. You give and they take. Can't you understand, I want to get away to somewhere where there's no one pushing us around and we can start really finding each other again?'

'Yes, but . . .'

'With you, there's always a "but", isn't

there? Work's so much more important than us.'

'I told you how it would be before we got married.'

'You didn't say I was only going to be allowed to have what was left of you after they'd grabbed all they wanted.'

He silently swore. If only Charlotte Tourkville had turned out to be the stuck-up bitch he'd expected to meet . . .

★   ★   ★

Noyes knew an inner revulsion because the sights and the smells took him back to his childhood, although not to any specific moment or setting. He wondered bitterly, angrily, why old age had to be a time of degradation. Tourkville had described Smith as large and very strong; now, he was a decaying wreck.

A DC from the local division had brought him to Smith's mean back-to-back. 'You'll remember me,' the DC said. 'I came and had a bit of a chat about the ship you were on—the *Waitawea*.'

'She's gone,' Smith said in his thin, quavery voice.

'Yeah, I know. Well, this is a friend of mine who'd like to ask you a few questions.'

Smith's face contorted and it was obvious that he was in considerable pain. He was dribbling and he used a torn and dirty handkerchief to wipe the corner of his mouth.

The DC looked at Noyes. Noyes, knowing he should experience compassion, but feeling only disgust, said: 'D'you remember how, when you were in the lifeboat, the fish came along?'

Smith mumbled: 'Are you a copper, same as him?'

'That's right, but I'm from Kent.'

'I don't remember nothing.'

'Not how the fish suddenly appeared and you caught some and squeezed liquid out of their flesh?'

He shook his head.

'I'm interested because I'm trying to help the cadet and his missus.'

He shook his head again.

'Look, Mr Smith, you don't need to worry—nothing can happen to you now.' That was a safe bet, thought Noyes; long before anything happened to anybody, Smith would be dead. 'The cadet might be in trouble, but if you'll tell me how the captain really died, I reckon to be able to help him out of it.'

'Don't know nothing.'

The DC tapped his forehead.

Noyes said: 'I don't believe the cadet had anything to do with the captain's death. You can tell me I'm right.'

There was no response.

'Is Andrews still alive?'

For a second, Noyes thought he saw fear in that pain-racked face. 'If Andrews is still alive, I can help the cadet . . . And I know that you didn't have anything to do with the captain's death.'

'Don't know nothing.'

'Let's move,' said the DC impatiently.

Either Smith was too sunk in pain and misery to remember anything, or he was too scared of the police to speak up; whichever, thought Noyes, it seemed that there was no point in continuing to question him.

*　　　*　　　*

Carol left the travel agent and slowly walked up Bank Street. For just over two hundred pounds each, they could have a one-bedroom flat overlooking the sea, with maid service; there was a large swimming-pool for the exclusive use of the tenants of the building; on the ground floor there was a café and a restaurant and a good meal would cost no more than five pounds; there was a great variety of food in the shops and it was all reasonably priced; a litre of perfectly drinkable wine was no more than fifty p; the sun shone all day, every day. The woman behind the counter had said that she went to the island every year and it was paradise.

Paradise . . . Pete would have to tell the

police that just for once they weren't going to have it all their own way—he was taking the leave due to him, period. She knew she'd flown off the handle with their last row, but hoped that once he'd cooled down, he'd understood what she'd really wanted to say. The happiness they'd originally known could be theirs again if only they worked to regain it. And if they were on holiday, so that novelty added excitement, they'd find the work easy.

She reached the shop where she worked and relieved the owner for lunch. As soon as she was on her own, she switched the outside line through to the telephone by the till and dialled divisional HQ. As she waited for the connection to be made, she rehearsed her lines. First the apology. She'd been a bitch. (But she'd let him know that she'd had cause to be—he'd begin to lose respect for her if she didn't fight back.) Then she'd tell him she loved him (in the nonsensical phrases which formed their private language). Finally, she'd persuade him to demand his time off. He could quote compassionate grounds; his wife's stress syndrome should sound good . . .

The call was answered. 'Would you put me through to DC Noyes, please?' She waited. The sea would be as blue as the travel posters suggested . . .

'I'm sorry, but he's not in the station.'

'Have you any idea when he'll be back?'

'I haven't, but I'll try and find out.'

There was a longer wait. Sunbathing by the pool . . .

'He won't be in at all today; he's on leave.'

Surprise made her speak abruptly. 'He certainly is not.'

'I've just spoken to the detective-sergeant. DC Noyes is on leave.'

'Will you put me through to Mr Burrow.' There were a couple of clicks before Burrow said: 'Detective-sergeant.'

'It's Carol. Where's Pete?'

'But . . .' There was a pause. 'Surely you know?'

'If I did, I wouldn't be phoning now. I've just spoken to the woman on the switchboard and all she can say is that Pete's on leave—but he left for work this morning as usual.' She waited. When nothing was said, she started to know an icy fear. 'Has something happened to him?'

'Not as far as I know.'

'Then where the hell is he?'

'But like I said, he started leave yesterday.'

'You're saying he didn't report in this morning?'

'That's right. But then we didn't expect him.'

Judy! All the time he'd gone on about not being able to take time off because of the workload, he'd been planning to meet that red-headed bitch. He was with her now, laughing because it had all been so easy . . .

She thanked Burrow, without explaining anything, replaced the receiver. Tears trickled down her cheeks. Angrily, she brushed them away. You bloody fool, she silently shouted at herself, remembering her fantasies about the holiday in the sun during which they'd rediscover each other . . .

CHAPTER TWENTY-TWO

As Noyes drove round the central flowerbed and away, Tourkville slammed the front door shut, then swung round. 'Why did you tell him everything?' he asked angrily.

'I had to,' Charlotte replied.

'Can't you understand what you've done?'

'Why did you pay that blackmail money?'

'Surely to God, that's obvious?'

'No. I know nothing about the law, but I do have reasonable common sense and even though the two sometimes don't go together, it did seem when you first told me enough of the truth roughly to understand what had happened that it would be extremely unlikely you would ever be charged with killing the captain. I asked Mr Noyes about it and he confirmed that. So you must have realized that whatever that beastly little man said, the odds were you wouldn't end up being tried and found guilty. Yet you meekly paid him money. Why?'

'Because . . .' He stopped.

'Well?'

'I was afraid that if the police questioned me, I'd be impelled to confess.'

'If there were no supporting evidence, a confession wouldn't have been enough. And why would you have confessed—to gain the absolution of punishment?'

'If you want to put it like that. I know that makes me sound soft . . .'

'No, Pierre, not soft; just unyielding like the oak tree which won't bend to the wind and so risks being blown down . . . But that's not the real answer.'

'Isn't it?'

'You knew that by paying out all that money you were putting land at risk and normally you'd do anything rather than that; certainly, you'd overcome any possible yearning for absolution. So what really made you give in to his filthy demands.'

He took hold of her hand and led the way into the green room. Releasing her, he continued on to the cocktail cabinet. 'What d'you want?'

'Whisky, please; a strong one.'

He poured out the drinks, handed her a glass, then stood with his back to the large fireplace. 'Remember what happened just

231

over a year ago?'

She thought back, but couldn't immediately remember any event which seemed relevant to the present context. 'What exactly?'

He drank. 'After the sitting MP for Lower Warren died suddenly, David was put on the shortlist of prospective Liberal candidates to succeed him.'

'Of course!' she exclaimed, beginning to see the answer to her original question.

'I reckoned that if I hit the headlines and all the circumstances of what went on in the boat were spelled out, David's chances of securing that adoption would inevitably drop to nil; no matter how unfairly, he'd become tarred by the facts. So I had to try and keep the story quiet.'

'Even if in doing so the estate was endangered?'

'Whatever the cost.'

She remembered the day she'd found him checking accounts in the library and she'd asked him to try to get on better with David and he, with a sudden anger that had puzzled her, had talked about it being too late. Only now did she realize what he had really meant. 'But by paying the blackmail money you've put it at risk.'

'I suppose you could say that that's a classic example of avoiding the sea monster but ending up in the whirlpool,' he said bitterly.

232

'The real trouble was that I was naïve enough to hope Gert was telling the truth when he said that if I paid him the five thousand he'd never come back for more.'

'But you knew the blackmailer always does come back.'

'Hope's stronger than logic.'

'What you're really saying is, you took the risk, knowing what it could cost, for David's sake?'

'I've always hoped we'd start to get on better together. But if he'd lost the chance of a safe seat, he'd never have forgiven me. He's so stubborn.'

'You're hardly the man to complain of stubbornness! Why the hell didn't you tell me all this a long time ago?' She walked forward until she stood immediately in front of him. 'Shall I confess something now?'

'Provided you don't look to me to grant absolution.'

'The saddest moments of my marriage have been when it seemed you didn't just not get on with David, you actually hated him.'

'There've been times when I've wondered if I do.'

'It's his brash rejection of so much of what you value that you hate; not him. You could never have risked so much if you'd hated him. Thank God I've learned that.' She kissed him on the cheek, then turned, went over to a chair, and sat. 'Pierre, you're going to prove something else, just as important. That you didn't kill the captain or have anything to do with his death.'

'How?'

'By doing as Mr Noyes suggested; by going to Portsmouth and talking to Smith.'

'Noyes is a trained interrogator, but he admitted that he couldn't get Daisy to say anything. So where's the point?'

'He explained. He suspects that Smith knows Andrews is alive, but isn't ever going to admit that to a policeman. You're nothing to do with the police; and since you and he sailed together, were torpedoed together, and survived together, there's a special bond between you which may persuade him to help . . . You've got to try. This could be your one chance to lift the nightmare.'

Lift it? he wondered. Or confirm it?

★   ★   ★

As he approached his house, Noyes noticed that the light in the hall wasn't on, but did not immediately see any significance in the fact; he assumed Carol had switched it off while she worked in one of the rooms. Aided by a nearby street lamp, he inserted the key in the front door, turned it, pulled open the door. He switched on the hall light. 'Carol,' he called out. There was no answer. He put the wrapped box of expensive chocolates on the hall table. They were a peace offering; a small recompense for a lost holiday in Tenerife.

When she went out unexpectedly, she always left a note on the kitchen table. There was one there now. He read it; swore. Why hadn't she ever been able to understand that Judy had never meant anything more than resisted temptation?

Back in the hall, he opened the drawer of the telephone table and brought out the small notebook in which were the numbers they most commonly used. He found the one he wanted, dialled it. Carol's mother was one of those soft-spoken, gentle women who smiled a lot, hated scenes, and nursed their dislikes; it had been quite a time before he'd learned that she'd warned Carol against marrying him because he came from a not very nice background.

She answered. 'Can I have a word with Carol, please,' he said.

'Who is that?'

She must have recognized his voice. But in her world, certain social conventions were always observed. 'It's Peter. Carol's husband,' he added sarcastically.

'But how nice to hear from you. How are you?'

'Living.' He should, he knew, now ask her how she was, but that would be to have to listen to a catalogue of trivial troubles.

'Would you put me through to Carol?'

'But she's not here.'

'Are you sure?'

'Well, of course I'm sure. I didn't know she was coming up to see me. She never said . . .'

'Do you know where she's gone?'

'I naturally imagined she was with you. Is something the matter?'

'Nothing's wrong.' He said a curt goodbye and rang off. That would give Mrs Gatling something to gossip about at her next bridge afternoon . . . Perhaps Carol was with Margery. Carol was not and Margery was sophisticatedly amused and said that when he got fed up with his own cooking to trot along and take pot luck with the Crosby family . . . Was she with Anne? There was no answer.

The note had concluded: '. . . so I'm going away. I don't suppose you'll give a damn where I've gone, but if you do, don't bother to try to find me because you won't succeed.' Then he was wasting his time in phoning anywhere where he might normally expect her to be.

He went through to the dining-room and poured himself out a large gin and tonic. Goddamn it, he thought bitterly, why was it that life always played such a sick joker? In the past, he'd always looked after number one because bitter experience had taught him that if he didn't, no one else would. Then, caught

236

up in an emotional relationship he couldn't define, he'd deliberately set out to help someone else at his own expense. His reward for such self-sacrifice turned out to be a hearty kick in the crutch.

★   ★   ★

Tourkville parked behind a battered Escort. He crossed the pavement, knocked on the front door of No. 7 and, when there was no answer, knocked again. He tried the handle and the door opened. The smell inside reminded him of the days when myxomatosis had ravaged the countryside for the first time and everywhere the air had been heavy with the stink of corruption. 'Anyone at home?' From the room on his right there came a muted, incomprehensible answer; a grossly fat cat suddenly shot up the stairs.

He would never have recognized Smith. Time and the fatal illness had stripped away the slightest resemblance to the tough man he'd once known. He introduced himself, sat.

'Doing all right, are you?' asked Smith, his rheumy eyes noting the cut of Tourkville's clothes.

'Not too badly.'

'I ain't.'

'I'm very sorry.' That was trite, thought Tourkville; but what else could he say? 'Does someone come in and help you?'

'The missus from next door. And then there's the nurse what calls . . .' He flinched. 'It's like something was gnawing inside me.'

Smith was waiting for the end; forty-five years ago they'd waited for the end in the drifting lifeboat, but then there had been that one chance in a thousand they'd be rescued. 'I've come to ask you to be kind enough to tell me something. How did the captain die?'

'You was there.'

'But I can't remember anything about those last days. My mind goes blank on me. How did he die?'

'What's it matter?'

'I must know.'

There was a long pause. 'Like the rest of 'em.'

'You're saying he died naturally?'

'Why not?'

'And the fish—did they return?'

''Course they did. How'd we catch more if they didn't?'

Perversely, he had to test the assurance which meant so much to him. 'Why did he die when he wasn't any weaker than the rest of us?'

'How'd I know?'

'Harwood said I killed him. And that the fish never returned. Was he lying?'

'Yes.'

'Why?'

'To make you pay.'

'Then you knew he was blackmailing me?'

Smith was silent.

'Was he blackmailing someone else as well?'

Smith suddenly flinched and groaned. After a while, he very slowly turned to his right and picked up two pills and a glass of water from the small table immediately by the side of the chair. The water rippled to the shaking of his hand as he drank and swallowed the pills.

'Is Andrews alive?'

'It was Mike's fault.'

'I don't understand what you mean.'

'He shouldn't've been so cruel.'

Tourkville listened to the halting, disjointed story. Harwood knew from bitter experience that he had to have a protector if he were to avoid the cruel persecution to which many of the crew would enjoy subjecting him and so he'd teamed up with Smith; but he was promiscuous and after a short while he'd tried surreptitiously to strike up a further friendship with Andrews. Nothing happened in the closed community of a ship without people learning about it. Smith was carefully informed of what was happening. But he didn't have to take any action. Andrews rejected Harwood with such verbal viciousness that Harwood never forgot it, even though it could have been only one rejection of many.

After the rescue, Smith and Harwood had signed on on the same ship and had continued to sail together until the war ended. Then they'd both gone ashore. Smith had found a solid but monotonous job which paid a regular wage; Harwood, ignoring Smith's pleas to stay, had left to look for an easy life. From time to time, when financially strapped, he'd returned and taken all he could get before leaving once more.

Just before Smith first fell ill, Harwood had arrived yet again. But this time he'd not come to sponge, he'd come maliciously to boast. He'd found himself a fortune. From now on he was going to live a rich man's life. (There was no suggestion that in his good fortune he'd repay Smith for all he'd received over the years.) Did Smith remember that cocky bastard, Mike, who was supposed to have been killed by a V-2? Well, he hadn't been. And now he was stinking rich, so he was going to have to pay through the nose if he wished to remain stinking rich . . .

Smith had told Harwood if he valued their friendship to forget the idea because it must lead to trouble. Harwood had laughed with contempt. Valued their friendship? Overvalued at a farthing. A great lumpy, ignorant, uncouth, ugly man with the manners and mind of a pig . . .

Tourkville judged that even now, when Smith was so close to death that an outsider would have imagined all past emotions had become meaningless, this final, contemptuous dismissal still bitterly hurt. But, by some strange stretch of illogical imagination, which turned the facts inside out and telescoped tens of years, he blamed Andrews for the heartless insults. 'Did Harwood tell you where Andrews is living now?'

Smith lay back in the chair, his eyes closed. 'Up in London,' he mumbled.

'Whereabouts exactly?'

There was silence.

'Did he say anything which suggested where?'

Smith still did not answer.

It was impossible to judge whether Smith knew something more and was not going to say what that was, or knew nothing. Then this was the end of the line. He'd learned that he was innocent of any involvement in the captain's death, since that had been natural, but had not obtained evidence which would help him prove once and for all that he knew nothing about Harwood's murder. Then he suddenly realized that because revenge was the most powerful of all motives, if Smith with complete illogicality blamed Andrews for his final rejection by Harwood, there was a chance of persuading Smith to speak up, if he did know something more. 'If I could find Andrews, it might become possible to prove that it was he who murdered Harwood.'

After a long while, Smith said: 'It's a rich man's house in Sommerstan Road.'

'Which part of London is that in?'

'He never said.'

'What name is Andrews using now?'

He shook his head.

Tourkville stood, said goodbye, and left, thankful to escape the dirt, the smell, the suffering, and the past. It was only as he drove away that he realized how premature was his intense relief over the fact that the captain had died a natural death. If that were true, how could Harwood have successfully blackmailed Andrews?

CHAPTER TWENTY-THREE

Noyes found it easier to identify the probable whereabouts of the Sommerstan Road in question than to persuade the detective-sergeant he spoke to to agree to his making inquiries without the assistance (supervision) of a member of the Metropolitan CID. There were in the Greater London area three Sommerstan Roads and one Sommerstan Avenue; these were situated in SW7, NW9, NW2, and SE15, and it was reasonable to suppose that a rich man would choose to live in SW7 in preference to the other localities. The detective-sergeant quoted rules and regulations and codes of practice and it was only after a third whisky at the nearby pub that he finally and reluctantly agreed to Noyes carrying on on his own.

Short and curving, Sommerstan Road contained twenty-five houses, all large, all with basements, all clearly the homes of the wealthy. How to discover which of the twenty-four belonged to Andrews? Tourkville had described him as four or five years older than himself—which made him sixty-fiveish—six-foot to six-one high, well built, noticeably handsome in a rugged manner, probably blue-eyed, light brown curly hair, very quick-growing beard, and left-handed. By chatting to nearby shopkeepers, a road sweeper, two delivery men, and a very chic au pair girl, Noyes narrowed the possible addresses down to two. At the first one, a tarted up woman with a supercilious manner and a drawling voice said her husband was in Bahrein, had been for the past seven weeks, and was not expected to return for another two. At the second house, a pleasant, friendly, well-dressed woman said her husband was at his office. He spun her a yarn and she provided him with the name and address of the office.

He caught a bus to Letchbourne Street, walked three parts down this to the high-rise concrete and glass block, went in. A lift took him up to the tenth floor and the offices of T.

& J. Roach. It was a name that had recently become familiar and almost immediately he remembered why. They were the advertising agency which had been engaged to pep up the image of the Conservative party before the next election. As far as he was concerned, they were wasting their time.

The large reception area was nearly as tastefully furnished as the blonde behind the desk. She regretted that Mr Kingham was very busy and unless he had an appointment . . . He showed her his warrant card. She used the internal telephone to speak to Kingham's private secretary and when the call was over told him that Mr Kingham would see him in a minute. He sat at a low table and leafed through a glossy magazine.

'I'm Mr Kingham's secretary, Mr Noyes. Would you like to follow me?'

He enjoyed following her; she rolled her bottom with sensuous grace.

Kingham did not stand, but his greeting was perfectly amiable. 'Good morning. Do sit down there.' He spoke with that slight extra care, that touch of deliberation, which suggested to a trained ear that he had once had a different accent.

Noyes sat on the chair set in front of the desk and studied Kingham. Sixty-fiveish, well built, a distinguished face, blue eyes, hair naturally wavy and now grey, a chin showing a five o'clock shadow although it was impossible to believe that he had not shaved that morning.

'I understand that you're making certain inquiries . . .' Kingham was interrupted by the telephone. With a quick word of apology, he lifted the receiver, listened, spoke briefly, replaced it. He was left-handed. 'What exactly is the nature of your inquiries? I'm sorry if I seem to rush you, but I do have an appointment quite soon.'

'I'll be as quick as I can, Mr Andrews.'

He answered calmly: 'I beg your pardon?

But Noyes had not missed the brief sense of shocked wariness. 'Your real name is Michael Andrews.'

'It is Kingham.'

'You were an ordinary seaman on the *Waitawea* on her last voyage during the war.'

'I have never sailed as an ordinary seaman on any ship at any time.'

'The *Waitawea* was torpedoed and the crew had to take to the boats; you were in the captain's. Thirty-four days later, you and the three other survivors were picked up by a Swedish ship.'

'I can only assume you have been seriously misled . . .'

'Do you have papers to prove you're Kingham and not Andrews?'

'Of course.'

'Were they stolen or bought?'

'This is becoming not only ridiculous, but

245

also annoying.'

'You'll remember the names of the other survivors—Cadet Tourkville, Harwood, and Smith. Aboard ship, the two stewards formed a turn, Gert and Daisy. Gert had taken a shine to you, but you didn't reciprocate his feelings and told him so in no uncertain manner. It's ironic how Smith—Daisy—has always blamed you for being so brutally frank that you shattered Gert's self-esteem. He also knows that you murdered Gert. Two reasons for doing all he could to identify you.'

'Your suggestions are absurd.'

'Not absurd, strange; but that's how people are.' Noyes paused, then said thoughtfully: 'Identity's a funny thing. Most times, it's not who you really are that matters, it's who other people believe you to be. So if the bank manager accepts your account in the name of John Smith, the postman delivers letters at your house addressed to John Smith, and the doctor treats you as John Smith, all the world assumes that that's who you are and nobody ever stops to question the fact. And to persuade the bank manager, the postman, and the doctor that you are who you claim to be, all you need are a few bits of paper that can easily be forged—birth certificate, medical card, possibly a letter of recommendation. Thereafter, no one demands that you prove your right to those bits of paper.'

'This is elementary and immaterial.'

'Just because something's elementary, it doesn't mean it's obvious, and as a matter of fact, it's very material. Really, it's all like the Emperor's new clothes—everyone agrees they're quite magnificent until one little boy points out that he isn't wearing any. Everyone is certain of John Smith's identity until someone says, prove it with history.'

'I don't think I can waste any more of my time listening to you.'

'Could you prove your present identity by history?'

'I've no dea what you mean.'

'Could you take me to the house where you were born, the school where you were taught, the barracks where you spent your first night in the army, assuming you were called up? Could you return to the sweetshop at the corner where the ancient old biddy would look up into your face and say, yes, she remembers selling you halfpenny packets of bubble gum when you were so high?'

'Any corner shop I patronized when I was young will have disappeared years ago.'

'As will the house where you were born. And the area will have been re-developed and all those who lived there will have been scattered to the four winds. Which is why you'll always be confident that if you have to, you'll make history support you. But you're forgetting one small dissenting voice from the

247

past.'

'What?'

'Your own voice. Do you remember what happened when you joined the Merchant Navy?'

'Since I never did, the answer is that it would be impossible.'

'The shipping company interviewed you, gave you a medical, and agreed to sign you on; then you were issued with a special seaman's identity card and on this were your fingerprints, a second set of which were taken for the records. For some reason known only to the bureaucrats, these are still held—perhaps fifty-odd years are as nothing to the loyal bureaucrat. As a result. I have only to take your fingerprints—either with your permission or after a court order, easily obtained since this is a murder case—and compare them with those on record to prove conclusively that you are the Michael Andrews who sailed on the *Waitawea*.'

Kingham studied Noyes carefully, trying to gauge whether this was a bluff; he found himself unable to do so, which meant he dared not presume it was. He searched for signs of a weakness he could exploit—perhaps a venality—but saw only strength. Characteristically, he came to a quick decision. 'It is no offence to change one's name when it is not done with intent to deceive for profit.'

'It is an offence to obtain or to use false documents; it is also an offence to change one's name in order to escape a charge of murder, although, of course, the lesser charge becomes overwhelmed by the greater.'

'There could never have been such a charge.'

'How did the captain die?'

'Naturally, if dying from thirst and exposure can be regarded as natural.'

'If that were the truth, you'd never have allowed Harwood to blackmail you.'

'No one has ever blackmailed me.'

'A search through all your financial affairs will show that in the past year you have exceptionally withdrawn something between seventy and ninety thousand pounds.'

'Impossible. In any case, why should anyone take either the time or the trouble?'

'To verify the motive for the murder.'

'I have just said, the captain died a natural death.'

'Harwood was murdered because he'd been blackmailing you.'

'As a matter of interest, supposedly on what grounds?'

'That the captain was killed in order that the rest of you should live.'

'How would his death have helped us?'

'Then you could use his flesh for bait to catch more fish, which had returned, as you had previously used the flesh of men who had died naturally.'

'Is that all?'

'Isn't that enough?' asked Noyes with angry astonishment.

'Yes, I suppose it is.'

What in the hell was he getting at? wondered Noyes, trying and failing to interpret the other's attitude.

When Kingham next spoke his voice once more expressed only self-assurance tinged with mockery. 'Presumably, Harwood claimed that Tourkville killed the captain. What's Tourkville's answer to that?'

'He can't remember what happened.'

'I suppose one could call that a fortunate and fortuitous amnesia.' Kingham stood, walked over to the nearer window and stared out at the street below, his hands clasped behind his back. 'One thing has to be remembered. Exposure, salt water boils, swollen cracked, blackened tongue, agonizing thirst, and a sense of total helplessness, can turn a man insane, not only in the normal sense, but also in the more restricted sense that he no longer thinks or acts as he would under normal conditions.' He turned, but remained standing by the window. 'After the captain's death, he was, of course, in command of the boat.'

'Perhaps *de jure*; but you were *de facto* in command ever since the bos'un died.'

'You sound as if that happened some time

before?'

'It did.'

'The bos'un died less than twenty-four hours before the captain.'

'Tourkville places his death at very much earlier.'

'Which shows that his mind was becoming confused before the rest of us fully realized that fact; and considering he was so young, that is hardly to be wondered at.'

'But your mind wasn't in the least bit confused, so you can tell me what really happened.'

'Of course. At the beginning, we'd waited for the captain to take command, but it became obvious that he'd abdicated. So the bos'un, naturally in the name of the captain—when dealing with the British, always plan a revolution in terms which can be declared legal—took over and kept us going until he died. Did Tourkville tell you about the first time the fish came?'

'Yes.'

'It was the bos'un, and by now not even in the captain's name, who said they'd never take the lures and we must use bait.'

'Tourkville swears it was you who gave the order to use human flesh.'

'With the bos'un there, I wasn't giving any orders . . . That kept us going for a little, but things soon became desperate again and eventually the bos'un died. I pointed out to

251

Tourkville that he simply had to get through to the captain and make him pull himself together; he tried again, said there wasn't a hope, and he'd have formally to take over.'

'You're saying you accepted a young cadet on his first trip as now being in command?'

'He wore epaulettes—as I said, we British always respect rank—so naturally we accepted his orders. In any case, he proved himself surprisingly competent.'

'According to Tourkville, it was you who gave all the orders.'

'You've mentioned that he can't remember details; he's right, he can't.'

'What happened when the captain died?'

'I don't know.'

'Your memory has also gone walkabout?'

'My memory's OK. I simply do not know.'

'Why not?'

'The fish returned and we tried to catch them, but without bait it was hopeless. Tourkville began to say that if one of us didn't die before the fish left us again, so that we'd have more bait, we'd all die. I tried to shut him up, because it was obvious what he was getting at, but it wasn't any use.

'When he realized none of us was going to do what he was trying to suggest, he went for'd and sat on the same thwart as the captain. Nothing happened and so we all lost interest, reckoning the cadet didn't know what he'd been saying. Then the captain

252

suddenly started moaning. He doubled up and fell to the boards, kicked a couple of times, and was dead.'

'What had killed him?'

'I've no idea.'

'You can guess.'

'The cadet had a knife in his hand which he then used to cut out the bait. That's all I can tell you.'

'Was there a wound in the captain's body?'

'There was blood around his waist.'

'You're suggesting Tourkville knifed him?'

'I'm suggesting nothing. You asked me for the facts, I've given them as I know them.'

'You're lying. You'd long since taken command and it was you who ordered bait to be used the first time; it was you who decided the captain had to die if the remaining four of you were to have the chance to live.'

Kingham returned to his chair and sat.

'If Tourkville had been in command and had killed the captain, Harwood wouldn't have been in a position to blackmail you.'

'As I've already said, I have never been blackmailed . . . But shall we suppose, for the sake of argument, that I was. Then within the boundary of such an assumption, I'll suggest both grounds for the blackmail and a reason for my paying it. After the captain died, we again used human flesh as bait and this time we caught a large number of fish which undoubtedly saved our lives. If such a

253

story came to light now, the sensational press would have a field day with it. Inevitably, such publicity would be extremely harmful to me and to my firm. In view of this, it would surely seem to be the lesser of two evils to pay for its suppression?'

'But blackmail never stops.'

'Is that a fact?'

'The blackmailer promises it's a once-and-for-all payment, but sooner or later—usually sooner—he comes back for more. Harwood came back five months later. You're more than smart enough to have known that that's how it would be . . . So why wait the whole year before putting out the contract that was designed to make his murder look like a drunken accident and would have done if executed more skilfully?'

'Obviously, I can't answer. The only contracts I have anything to do with are, thankfully, far less lethal.'

'You can't offer another supposition?'

'I suppose I could suggest that I might have remembered the old adage that if you give a man enough rope, he'll hang himself. He was a poofter, old but still ambitious, even if performance couldn't live up to it. So the odds had to be that if he had hard money, he'd start entertaining young men in a big way. And that always opens up the possibility of one of them—from contempt as much as greed—robbing and killing him. So by

254

feeding him money, I'd be ensuring there'd be such a plethora of suspects, many of whom would never be traced, that I'd completely obscure my own involvement in events . . . Now, tell me something; why are you bothering with all this?'

'By your standards, are two murders of too little significance to worry about?'

'However zealous, surely you'll agree that not every murder is of the same degree of heinousness? The captain died forty-five years ago, so it's history; in any case, he'd betrayed every other man aboard and he deserved to die. And Harwood, according to you, tried his hand at blackmail. The world's very well rid of him as well.'

'Not in the eyes of the law.'

'The law has boundaries, life doesn't; that's why the law often is, as Dickens observed, an ass.'

'Ass or not, no one is above it.'

'But perhaps beyond it when there are only two surviving eye-witnesses?'

'Three.'

'Then you didn't read yesterday's *Telegraph*. In it there was a very brief paragraph reporting the death of Sidney Smith, one of only four survivors of the TSS *Waitawea* who were adrift in a lifeboat for a record thirty-four days. In fact, thirty-four days didn't constitute a record, but no matter . . . So now there are only two witnesses to

255

events and one of those claims to have no memory of them. Or to put it in another way, only my evidence can be accepted and I think you'll have to agree that therefore any attempt to dredge up the past can only adversely affect Tourkville. Is that a development that you'd welcome?'

Noyes stood. 'There's one last question. Why did you put Harwood on to Tourkville?'

'Yet another supposition? Very well. While Harwood initially had no idea of Tourkville's social and financial position in life, I did—through cattle, funnily enough. So I knew that he'd been born into privilege. I most definitely had not. I've had to fight my way right up from the bottom. So if I was going to have to suffer for a while, why shouldn't he do the same for once? No, that's wrong—for a second time.

'Incidentally, just before you go there's one more point you might like to consider. After our rescue, we were interviewed by officials from the Board of Trade—or was it called the Ministry of War Transport by then? They were studying survivals at sea to learn if anything more could be done for those who had to take to boats or rafts. When I was questioned, I took the opportunity to emphasize that, young and inexperienced as he was, and even though his mind had become confused in certain respects, the cadet had taken command of the lifeboat and

256

shown exceptional powers of leadership; and it was solely due to him that we survived. My evidence will still be on record. So it might be difficult to claim now that it was really I who was in command and who gave the orders.'

Even then, thought Noyes, when one would have expected him merely to wallow in the pleasure of survival, he'd been smart enough to appreciate the need to protect himself. Noyes turned and walked across to the door, conscious of the mocking expression on Kingham's face.

*   *   *

He left Plaistow tube station and walked down South Staffs Street. Three versions (or rather, two and a blank) of the same event—the captain had died naturally; the captain had died suddenly, with Tourkville by his side, knife in hand; no memory of how the captain had died. There was no hard evidence to say which was the correct version, but he surely had to accept that if it were held the captain had been murdered, only Tourkville could be charged, if anyone was. What about the murder of Harwood? It had been a contract job in which one or more professionals had been employed. No evidence had come to light to identify who they were and it was likely that none now would. There was a chance in a hundred that identifying Kingham to the police in Etrington would gain the lead they needed, but then inevitably reference must be made to the captain's death. If Kingham had been clever enough to hide his payments of the blackmail money—and it was difficult to believe he hadn't—then that would leave Tourkville exposed; and he had originally been, and to some extent still was, a suspect because of the circumstantial evidence . . . The law demanded Harwood's murderer be found. But did justice?

He reached No. 74, an old, large, brickbuilt building, washed with industrial pollution. A brass plate, newly polished, named the Sir Alan Bennet Merchant Navy Museum.

It was obviously not a popular museum and in view of its situation and the dull displays this was hardly surprising. He asked an elderly attendant where he'd find the log book of the cadet from the *Waitawea* and was shown a glass-topped cabinet, inside which was an exercise book, opened so that one could read the pencil entries on two of the badly stained pages.

'I'd like to look through the rest of the book,' he said.

The attendant shook his head. 'It's got to stay in the cabinet.'

He showed his warrant card. The attendant left, soon returned with a key with which he unlocked the cabinet. He picked out the exercise book and handed it over.

Noyes skimmed through the entries. Deaths were listed after weather, wind, and sea. The bos'un had died on the eleventh day. Here was proof that in one detail at least, Tourkville had told the truth, Kingham had lied . . . He turned back to the beginning and now read slowly. Initially, the writing was firm, the entries precise. Then, with increasing rapidity, the writing became a scrawl and the entries fragmentary.

Imagination lifted him into the lifeboat. He knew the brutality of the burning sun; the terror of seeing the first water container emptied; the wild anger as the thieving steward spilled the contents of a water beaker; the agonizing drift into death which all of them would have made but for an ordinary seaman whose qualities were so extraordinary that he had made them go on fighting . . .

He handed the book back.

The attendant carefully replaced it in the case, open at the same two pages as before. 'I was at sea in them days. I know what it was like.'

'I'm beginning to learn,' replied Noyes.

CHAPTER TWENTY-FOUR

Tourkville stood in front of the fireplace in the green room; Charlotte stepped closer to him until she could reach down and grip his hand.

Noyes, who had just sat in one of the armchairs, looked up at them and said: 'I'm afraid I haven't been able to find and identify Andrews.'

Charlotte could feel the beads of sweat form on the palm of her husband's hand.

'You're saying then, that I'll never know if my memory cut out because of something it doesn't want to remember . . .' began Tourkville.

'I'm saying nothing of the sort. Your memory cut out because of all you'd suffered and were suffering.'

'Then what . . . what about the captain?'

'Smith told you the truth when he said the captain died from natural causes.'

'How can you be certain it was the truth?'

'Smith knew he was on the point of dying and it's accepted that when a man acknowledges that, he does not lie.'

'If that's the truth, how could Andrews have been open to blackmail?'

'Like you, I wondered about that. I reckon to have the answer. Andrews was older than you and therefore mentally much tougher so the suffering didn't scramble his mind. Harwood couldn't feed him the lie that he'd murdered the captain. But even so, Harwood had a big handle. This all pivots around the fact that we know Andrews must now be a very rich man and probably in a position, perhaps both socially and financially, where any sort of scandal could hit him hard. If the facts ever came out that he'd once suggested using the flesh of dead men as bait, he'd be bang in the middle of a scandal because there are always hypocrites eager and willing to tear at the feet of anyone who's got more than they have. Andrews was paying to prevent the truth being published. Just as you were paying to prevent a lie being published.'

'Did he kill Harwood?'

'On the face of things, it seems a distinct possibility that he arranged to have Harwood murdered. But it's no more than a possibility. Harwood, despite his age, was still entertaining young men and any one of them might have killed him, either from perverse contempt or in the hopes of easily stealing something worthwhile.'

Charlotte said: 'But you're satisfied that Pierre didn't kill him?'

'Quite satisfied, Mrs Tourkville, that your husband didn't kill either Harwood or the captain.'

A few minutes later, as Noyes drove off,

Tourkville closed the front door.

'The nightmare's over,' she said, in a voice that was far from steady.

The nightmare was over. Now he could remember without fear; and look forward with hope. Because he'd paid the blackmail money, financially the estate was troubled, but following a second visit from himself and his accountant the bank manager had shown more sympathy than he had originally and had persuaded his head office to be more flexible. So, granted a little luck, successful economies, reasonable harvests (and silence from the Common Market), it should be possible to repair the financial damage without having to sell Dower Farm. Then, when David inherited . . .

'What are you thinking, Pierre?'

'That with luck I'll be able to hand on the estate as it is now. Then it'll be up to David what he does with it.'

'He'll work as hard as you to preserve it.'

'I still wonder. You seem so certain his attitude will change . . .'

'Without the need to fight you, he'll be able to allow himself that luxury, won't he?' She smiled. 'And by the time he inherits I hope he'll be very much older and more mature; he'll have learned that the future lies in the past.'

'Isn't that asking a bit too much, intellectually, of any Member of Parliament?'

262

She stepped forward, clasped her hands behind his neck, pulled his head down slightly so that she could kiss him. 'Rosalind says that sometimes you can be a really annoying old B. She's right!'

★   ★   ★

The front door of his house was unlocked, yet Noyes was certain he had locked it when he left that morning. He gently pushed it open, knowing the hinges would not squeak. From upstairs came the sounds of someone moving about.

He tiptoed across to the stairs and ascended them, carefully keeping to the centre of the carpet. Then, as he stepped on to the landing, he heard a woman say, 'Blast!' and recognized Carol's voice.

She was in their bedroom, looking through the right-hand built-in cupboard, and because her back was to the doorway, she did not know he was there. 'Forgotten something?' he asked.

She screamed as she whirled round. 'Goddamn it, you've just frightened a year off my life.'

'I'm sorry.'

She regained her poise. 'And I'm even sorrier that I made the mistake of deciding that at this time of the day there wouldn't be any fear of running into you.'

'Why not?'

'Because I reckoned you'd be too bloody busy.'

'It's finished with, at last . . . You know, it's funny but it never once occurred to me that you might find out I'd taken my leave by trying to get hold of me at the station.'

'Suppose it had, what would you have done? Asked the others to cover for you? And they would have. You lot always stick together and to hell with the old cows at home.'

He could not prevent himself yawning.

'Been having a heavy time? They always say that men dream of meeting a nymphomaniac, but soon buckle at the knees if they ever succeed.' Her hard sophistication suddenly cracked and when she next spoke there was pain in her voice. 'For God's sake, why couldn't you at least have been straight and told me what you were intending? Didn't you think you even owed me that much?'

'I knew you were so set on going to Madeira . . .'

'Tenerife. For a second honeymoon. Instead of which, it's a first divorce back here.' She began to cry.

He took a pace forward.

'Forget the corn,' she said violently. 'Still hoping a hug and a few soft words will let you play both games at once? You just don't know anything about me, not even after five years of marriage. You can't understand that with me it has to be all or nothing.'

'Like the girl in *Oklahoma!*' he said wearily.

'*Annie Get Your Gun*. Can't you get anything right?'

'It wouldn't seem like it, would it? Look, I know I ought to have told you what was happening, but I just didn't have the courage and that's being straight. You were so set on getting away that I reckoned if I said I couldn't make it, you'd blow your top.'

'Did you hope, then, that eventually I'd share you with that red-headed bitch?'

'Why bring her into it?'

'Because you've been with her all this time. Unless you've found yourself someone a bit fresher; and from all accounts, that wouldn't be difficult.'

'I haven't seen her since that time at the pub.'

'And I'm descended from Queen Victoria.'

'From when my leave started, I've been up in London, continuing inquiries into the Tourkville case. Burrow wouldn't allow any more time to it because the murder is Etrington's pigeon and what happened forty-five years ago in a lifeboat in the South Atlantic is forgotten history. Forgotten history for everyone but Tourkville and his wife. She was going crazy with worry.'

'You mean . . . You're saying you've given

up your leave to help her?'

'I couldn't stand seeing the awful look of desperation on her face.'

'So it *was* another woman!' She came forward until she stood immediately in front of him. 'D'you know something, Pete? This is the first time I've ever seen you fight someone else's battle . . . Maybe things are changing and I've been too blind to see it until now.'

He knew fierce hope. 'So suppose I buy a bottle of Spanish red and we sit under the sun lamp and make believe we're in Tenerife?'

Photoset, printed and bound in Great Britain by REDWOOD BURN LIMITED, Trowbridge, Wiltshire